GARTH ST OMER
January 1931.
Roman Catholic hig
seven years, 1949
Caribbean. He entered the University College of the West Indies, Jamaica, in 1956 on a UCWI scholarship, and graduated in 1959 with an Honours degree in French, with Spanish as subsidiary subject. Between 1959 and 1961 he taught as an English Language Assistant in *lycées* in Dax and Albi, France. From 1961 to 1966 he taught French and English at Apam Secondary School, Ghana. The years 1966 to 1969 were devoted to full-time writing of fiction, in England and the West Indies. In 1969 he entered the graduate school of Fine Arts of Columbia University, taking courses in creative writing, translation, film-making, film history and film aesthetics. He graduated in 1971 with the MFA degree. In 1971 he enrolled in the Comparative Literature programme of Princeton University to read for the PhD degree. He successfully completed the requirements in 1975, his dissertation being on *The Colonial Novel*, a comparative study of Albert Camus, V. S. Naipaul and Alejo Carpentier (Ann Arbor, Michigan: University Microfilms, 1975). In 1975 he joined the English Department of the University of California, Santa Barbara, as Associate Professor, and was subsequently promoted to the rank of full Professor. His awards include a Writing Grant from the Arts Council, London, England (1967), a Columbia University fellowship (1969–71), a Ford Foundation fellowship (1969–73), and a Princeton University fellowship (1971–75).

GARTH ST OMER

THE LIGHTS ON THE HILL

HEINEMANN

Heinemann Educational Books Ltd.
22 Bedford Square, London WC1B 3HH

Heinemann Educational Books (Nigeria) Ltd.
PMB 5205, Ibadan
Heinemann Educational Books (Kenya) Ltd.
Kijabe Street, PO Box 45314, Nairobi
Heinemann Educational Books Inc.
70 Court Street, Portsmouth, New Hampshire, 03801, USA
Heinemann Educational Books (Caribbean) Ltd.
175 Mountain View Avenue, Kingston 6, Jamaica

EDINBURGH MELBOURNE AUCKLAND HONG KONG
SINGAPORE KUALA LUMPUR NEW DELHI

© Garth St Omer 1968
First published by Faber and Faber Ltd, 1968
Photograph Garth St Omer courtesy Faber and Faber Ltd.
First published in Caribbean Writer's Series as CWS 35, in 1986

British Library Cataloguing in Publication Data

St. Omer, Garth
   The lights on the hill.—(Caribbean
   writers series; 35)
   I. Title   II. Series
   813[F]   PR6069.A426

   ISBN 0–435–98964–2

Printed in Great Britain by
Cox & Wyman Ltd, Reading

INTRODUCTION

When Garth St Omer was an undergraduate at the University College of the West Indies in Jamaica, which provided the setting for *The Lights on the Hill*, Colin Wilson's *The Outsider* (London, 1956), a study of twentieth-century alienation and world-weariness, was in the flower of its short-lived fame. Stephenson, the central character of *Lights*, bears all the marks of the Outsider.

Like St Omer, he enters university comparatively late, a fact which contributes to the sense of marginality which had been fostered in him from boyhood, beginning with his dubious paternity, the illegitimacy of his begetting, and the socio-economic deprivation of his mother and foster-mother. It is little wonder that the boy who had been nicknamed 'white nigger' by his peers should become the young man who characterizes himself to his fellow student Eddie as '[a]lways restless, always dissatisfied, hovering on the fringe of things, avoiding the centre or the depths' (ch. 1). Stephenson conforms to the idea of the Outsider even in his peripatetic habit. He likes to go for solitary, ruminative walks. This walking is aimless. It underlines his essential condition of stasis. He never walks towards, only around, on the periphery, away from.

In his role of Outsider, Stephenson is like others of St Omer's central characters. *Lights* was first published together with another novella, *Another Place Another Time*, in a volume entitled *Shades of Grey* (London, 1968). Although each of the two stories can stand entirely by itself, they are mutually illuminating and may indeed be read together as one novel.

Despite nominal and relatively superficial differences, their two protagonists—Stephenson of *Lights*, and the schoolboy Derek Charles of *Another Place*—are versions of the typical St Omer anti-hero as he has evolved through St Omer's various books, from *A Room on the Hill* (London, 1968), through *Shades of Grey*, to *Nor Any Country* (1969) and *J—, Black Bam and the Masqueraders* (1972).

The continuity of interest linking these works is suggested superficially by, among other things, the fact that two of the titles first occurred as phrases in preceding stories: 'another place, another time' occurring towards the end of *Lights*, which precedes its companion-piece in *Shades*, and 'nor any country' occurring at the end of *Another Place Another Time*— 'He had no cause nor any country now other than himself' (*Shades*, pp. 222–3). Besides, the same characters figure in more than one story. For instance, Peter Breville, who has a small, shadowy but significant role in *Lights*, turns up again as protagonist of *Nor Any Country* and co-protagonist of *J—, Black Bam and the Masqueraders*. It could be said, then, that St Omer's books together constitute the continuing non-saga of the St Omer anti-hero; and the volume title *Shades of Grey* would be a not inappropriate title for the entire *oeuvre*.

The St Omer protagonist is male, young, born and raised on a small island modelled on the novelist's native St Lucia. He is born into an environment of urban poverty or deprivation and into a family that is either broken or incapable of functioning as a sustaining source of moral and psychological authority for him, 'supported by no weight of tradition or lineage' (*Lights*, ch. 9). However, by virtue of his academic ability, and spurred on by an ambition encouraged by his parent(s), he is able to get and make good use of secondary education. He thereby puts himself into a position where there is a distinct possibility of his breaking out of the claustrophobic cell of island life to which he would otherwise be doomed, of achieving 'success' and 'independence' and so compensating for the deprivation and degradation of his beginnings.

In some cases he does manage to escape and gain a certain social status. In other cases, chance and circumstance thwart him, as they thwart Stephenson, in his attempt to achieve his ambition for status, independence and material security. But even where he does physically escape from his island and improve his social and material position, at a psychological level he never escapes. His alert, questioning and sensitive mind has been so deeply affected by his formative experiences that he carries his prison with him, inside him, wherever he goes. Stephenson, thwarted at first, does manage a kind of escape, but it is a case of too little too late.

So the primary drama of St Omer's fiction is a drama of self-consciousness and self-scrutiny, one in which the other characters are important to the protagonist insofar as they contribute to the process of his self-realization, and attractive in proportion as they seem to offer the possibility of that self-transcendence which he craves, although he may not be fully aware of these considerations.

His is a prison of paradox and contradiction. Stephenson's very desire for freedom and independence is counterpointed by a suspicion that man is essentially without freedom to determine the direction of his life, that anything but acceptance of whatever happens is self-delusion. The obsessive, clinical questioning and self-scrutiny, which signify a kind of intellectual freedom, are at the same time inseparable from the paralysis of will that afflicts Stephenson. His rigorous pursuit of honesty and truth, his abhorrence of self-deception, goes hand in hand with a sensitivity and a fear of exposure, disappointment and hurt which cause him to resort to lying and concealment. Craving self-transcendence, he seems nevertheless reluctant to part with a certain masochistic self-indulgence. And in the very moment, at the end of the story, of acknowledging 'that human effort, in the end, if it did not benefit others, was futile' (ch. 9), he is deciding to be 'alone again, working to benefit no one but himself', 'committed to his pursuit of futility' (ch. 9).

Ultimately, the view of life which Stephenson arrives at at

the end of *Lights*, a view which is more complicated and problematic than any formulation of it which he articulates, seems consonant with the definition of existentialism as given by the COD:

> an anti-intellectualist philosophy of life holding that man is free and responsible, based on the assumption that reality as existence can only be lived but can never become the object of thought.

This, paradoxically, in spite of Stephenson's protestation that man is not free, and in spite of his compulsion to make his life the object of thought. At any rate, his story may be read as a philosophical inquiry constructed in terms of the questions implicit in that definition.

Stephenson's suspicion that life is only a game, absurd, meaningless (Eddie's untimely death, the shrieks from the lunatic asylum), is painful particularly because it is the fear of someone driven by the 'will to meaning', someone in whom a sense of what the psychiatrist Viktor Frankl calls 'the existential vacuum' has been provoked by a frustration of that will to meaning (see *Encounter*, vol. 33, Nov. 1969). In any event, 'interpretation' of the St Omer protagonist is problematic because the experience of closely reading through the novels makes it difficult to take any of his seemingly definitive perceptions of life as being final and absolute for him, or as being completely true to his own experience.

Is Stephenson's indecisiveness, or his 'decision' to live entirely to and for himself, the logical result of a conclusively arrived at, even if wrong, philosophical position; or is the philosophical position a rationalization after a decision motivated by fear, or some chronic temperamental inadequacy, or whatever other reason? The St Omer protagonist has a self-indulgent capacity for thinking himself into a corner. But whatever his true motives, critics who read him simply as an exponent and embodiment of nihilism might re-consider him in the light of Frankl's observation that 'contrary to widely-held opinion, existentialism is not to be identified as contemporary nihilism'. Frankl argues that 'the true message of existentialism is not *nothingness*, but the *no-thingness* of man' (*op. cit.*, p. 52). Despite the pessimism and sense of futility associated with the 'existential vacuum', the individual's awareness of the vacuum is not nihilism, but a manifestation of the human-ness of man, an assertion of his will to preserve that in him which makes him a special kind of being not to be confused with any other.

In considering the question of whether the *person-hood* of the St Omer protagonist is preserved, one must consider the related question of whether the novelist's realization of the character as individual is made subservient to the realization of the social environment which produces the character and against which he reacts. One reviewer of *Shades*, by way of expressing dissatisfaction with the book, wrote: 'I feel blackmailed where the status of the ego is *essentially* jeopardized and the documentation tied to some cruelly urgent social problem' (Kathleen Nott, in *The Observer*, 15 Dec. 1968, p. 28).

It is not clear why the exploration of the ego should not be 'tied to some cruelly urgent social problem', but to hear that 'the status of the ego' is 'jeopardized' in *Shades* is surprising. Stephenson is not merely an illustration of a set of social problems nor a mere victim of history, even if he, at times, would like to think so. Another reviewer corrects the misreading when, speaking of Stephenson's predicament, he says: 'How much it is his fault and how much that of the society in which he is born is a nice question' (Richard Lister, *Evening Standard*, 9 Dec. 1968).

Stephenson's individuality of temperament is impressed on the reader's consciousness before we know fully the personal history and social circumstances which have conditioned and which 'excite' that temperament. And when we know them, they do not completely explain or explain away all his specific choices of action or inaction. Something is left over that is open to varying interpretations which cannot be finally resolved.

St Omer, then, manages carefully the business of examining the relationship between social forces and individual personality. He defines vividly but economically the 'hampering, threadlike pressures' (to use George Eliot's phrase) of West Indian 'small-island' life, especially on the underprivileged. At the same time, we see how the almost totally negative and pessimistic view of the island held by a Stephenson is determined by the constraints and limitations of his position and point of view. The gradual, piecemeal, seemingly unpremeditated disclosure of Stephenson's socio-economic background, culminating in the more sustained narrative outpouring in chapter 8, constitutes part of the novella's structural interest.

Carefully selected detail, uncluttered by comment, encapsulates the history of the island and its impact on the individual. Take, for example the incident recalled in chapter 8, when the boy and his foster-mother watch in helpless horror as a policeman is savagely beaten in the street by black American sailors stationed on the island during the Second World War. The episode enacts the traditional vulnerability and enforced subservience of colonial, third-world peoples and the exploitative brutality practised by the economically superior power. The fact that it is a policeman who is beaten signifies the pathetic lack of real power and authority among the petty authority figures of the boy's class.

The 'impotence' of the policeman is a version of the 'impotence' and 'absence' of fathers in the world of boys like Stephenson. The incident dramatizes for the boy, long before he experiences it fully at first hand, the idea of an apparently invincible 'system' which oppresses persons such as him. The fact that nobody goes to the assistance of the policeman may also suggest a supine acquiescence, a cowardice, on the part of the victimized, which will foster in the protagonist a certain contempt for them.

One important way by which St Omer delineates the limiting social pressures which beset Stephenson is by his portrayal of women. If the essential action of the work is the movement of Stephenson's consciousness and conscience, this movement is charted to a large extent in terms of his relationships with women. Most of these women are themselves the victims of those social forces which Stephenson wishes to escape, and so they (the women) represent the threat of those forces to Stephenson. To escape the 'stranglehold' of island life is to escape, among other things, the casual, sordid routine of cheap, furtive sex represented by the whores and easy women of his hometown, and by Edith, Rosa and Moira on the neighbouring island.

But even while seeing the sordid sexual routine for what it is, Stephenson allows himself to drift into it, partly for the fleeting pleasure and diversion which it provides, but also because it affords him the perverse satisfaction of hitting back at the society, through the cold, loveless, even brutal manner in which he exacts his pleasure from the women who embody so much of what he abhors in the society. So, for instance, his contempt for the hypocrisy, the soiled petty gentility and prudery of Rosa and her sister Edith is expressed in the way in which he uses Rosa sexually. 'At first she pretended to resist. Then she opened her legs and clasped him to her. He left the marks of his shoes all over the white sheet' (ch. 2). It is somewhat ironic to hear him say, reflecting on his affair with Rosa, that she 'had made him feel a little used' (ch. 3). The theme of sexual violence runs through St Omer's work, with the women as victims, as the men vent on them the fury of their frustration and sense of entrapment. The invariably broken or maimed or brutalized sexual relationships are a metaphor of the general social condition.

In general, women fare badly in St Omer's stories, not just because they are shown mostly, albeit with compassionate understanding, as downtrodden victims of the society which the novelist criticizes, but also because they are conceived in a very limited way in relation to the male protagonist. They appear to have a relatively narrow radius of being, so to speak. Their 'centre of self' is defined mostly in terms of their attachment to the protagonist. They exist only to the extent that they contribute to, or exacerbate, or are able to provide some relief from his *angst*. They themselves lack the complexity that would allow them the sophistication of a similar *angst*.

Thea is not so much an individual as an idea. She attracts Stephenson because she represents a kind of life which seems to be in direct contrast to that which he is trying to escape. Marie is the most intriguing and refreshing, because the least simplified, of the women in *Lights*. We may feel, from the time when we first see her, that she is intended to be merely another pathetic female victim—'the fat woman standing before the door of the car, her lower lip trembling, her hand, the black handbag hanging from the forearm, against her abdomen' (ch. 5). However, she resists reduction into a simple formula. This may have something to do with the fact that she is comparatively non-essential to the plot and is free of any sexual involvement with Stephenson.

By her unexpected re-entry, revenant-like, into Stephenson's life, bringing with her the knowledge about his past which he seeks to conceal, Marie serves, like the appearance of Carlton and the presence of the Brevilles on the campus, to dramatize the idea that, although Stephenson 'can't go home again', he can never escape from the past. His process of trying to understand himself and make sense of his life involves a seemingly obsessive engagement with the past, with memory. The nature of this engagement is reflected in the most immediately striking feature of St Omer's narrative technique, the recurrent use of time-shifts whereby the protagonist's consciousness is forever slipping back into memory. The contemplation of the present invariably turns into a recall of the past, in such a way as almost to blur the conventional distinction between present and past. The technique goes beyond what is normally denoted by the term 'flashback'.

When, in chapter 8, Stephenson sets out to give Thea a comprehensive account of his past, he expresses a perception of the structure of his narrative which constitutes an accurate and illuminating comment on the narrative structure of *Lights* itself:

> Even if she had not repeatedly interrupted to ask 'Why?' he would have needed to go back a step behind each action or phase of the life he was describing to her. In this way he was retracing, like a traveller going back along the line of imprints of his feet in sand, the events he had lived. It seemed, as he related them, that no single part of the recital was complete without what preceded or followed it. And so, after a while, he broke off his disjointed, interrupted and backward-moving narrative and began instead from the beginning.

But the linear narrative which then ensues, soon slips back, however briefly, into the 'disjointed, interrupted and backward-moving' mode.

In terms of the overall plot of *Lights*, this mode helps to elicit and maintain the reader's curiosity towards the eventual disclosure of Stephenson's crime and arrest. But its more important effect is to represent the activity of mind of a person intensely caught up by the need to make sense of his life. Caught between the hope of finding some purposive direction in that life, some logical connection between each 'part of the recital' and 'what preceded or followed it', and the fear that there is no such relationship between events, that all is accidental, arbitrary, meaningless, he seems to arrive at the view that, even if there is no 'meaning' in the conventional sense, the sheer relentless continuity of that life constitutes its own meaning and validity. Each event has its place because each serves to define the life, each is a part of the totality that constitutes that particular, unique life.

> No crisis, no disappointment, nothing that had happened to him had stopped the flow of his life. Like a river overcoming all opposition, merely by its inherent fluidity, it rolled on. Always it found its own channel, its own level. (ch. 9).

FURTHER READING

Edward Baugh, 'Since 1960: Some Highlights', in Bruce King (ed.), *West Indian Literature* (London, 1979), pp. 78–94 (85–7).

Michael Gilkes, 'Garth St Omer', *The West Indian Novel* (Boston, 1981), pp. 102–15.

Patricia Ismond, 'The St Lucian Background in Garth St Omer and Derek Walcott', *Caribbean Quarterly*, vol. 28, nos 1 & 2 (March–June 1982), pp. 32–43.

Jacqueline Kaye, 'Anonymity and Subjectivism in the Novels of Garth St Omer', *Journal of Commonwealth Literature*, vol. 10, no. 1 (August 1975), pp. 45–52.

Gerald Moore, 'Garth St Omer', in *Contemporary Novelists*, ed. James Vinson (London and New York, 1976), pp. 1188–91.

F. Gordon Rohlehr, 'Small Island Blues: A Short Review of the Novels of Garth St Omer', *Voices*, vol. 2, no. 1 (Sept.–Dec. 1969), pp. 22–8.

John Thieme, 'Double Identity in the Novels of Garth St Omer', *Ariel*, vol. 8, no. 3 (July 1977), pp. 81–97.

For Mr Lowe who once befriended me

Irresolute and proud,
I can never go back.
                    DEREK WALCOTT
How like a winter my absence has been
From thee,
            SHAKESPEARE

PART ONE

I

"What are you thinking of?" Thea asked him.

"Nothing," he answered.

"I knew it. One would think I should have learnt by now. Yet every time I ask the same question."

"And every time I give the same answer?"

"Yes, every time. How many times have I asked that question in two years I wonder?"

He did not answer.

"Do you think you could tell me?"

"How should I know?"

"Of course. You wouldn't. You don't even hear me sometimes."

"Now. You mustn't exaggerate."

"You must keep your secrets very well."

"I have no secrets."

His back was on the ground and his hands were under his head. The stars moved quickly, in formation, against the sky. He looked again and the illusion was gone. It was the clouds that moved briskly under the stars fixed above them. Below the clouds, in the distance, far away, clusters of dancing lights clung to the mountain top. Tonight, because of the moon, they were less bright.

"Of course you have secrets. Everyone has secrets."

"Do you?"

"Not for you, no. But for others I have secrets."

"I'd like to know everybody's secrets."

"And keep yours."

He looked at her and smiled. He thought again how lucky he was. But he said nothing to her. He wondered what she would have said if, in answer to her question about his thoughts, he had answered, "I am thinking again how inadequate I really am."

She would certainly expostulate, deny that he was inadequate. She would have to, for her own sake.

Or suppose he had said to her, "I was thinking again how nothing holds me now. How nothing compels my attention nor my interest. How even you can hold me for so long only."

He thought she might accept this answer more readily because of the element of strangeness his words might convey.

He laughed.

"What is it now?" she asked.

"Nothing," he said. And he laughed again.

"Of course."

"I just wondered why we ever take ourselves seriously."

"You mean why you do."

"But I don't," he said. "I used to but I don't any more. Don't you know that?"

"Do you know," she said, "that after nearly two years I know almost nothing about you?"

She added, "Except what I have seen here."

"Anyhow," he said, "I don't take myself seriously any more."

"That's why you're always thinking about nothing," she said. "You and I know it isn't nothing at all."

He smiled and finished lighting his cigarette.

"Light one for me too," she said.

"What is it then," he asked when they were smoking, "if it isn't nothing?"

"No," she said, "not tonight."

They smoked quietly for a while. In the valley below them, between the stunted trees away from the rocky bed where the river flowed now only when it rained, two cars, their lights out, were parked. A line of white ran downhill almost to the valley floor. It was the dirt road leading from the pitched one that continued somewhere at the top of the slope behind them.

"Come back," she said.

He joined the game. He had learnt to play it.

"I'm here," he said, "right here with you."

"Do you hear the wind?"

"No."

"Listen."

After a pause she asked, "You hear it?"

He heard it now. Then he did not hear it any more but could only feel it on his face.

"I don't hear it any more."

"But you feel it now, though?"

"Yes," he said, "I can feel it on my face."

"That's how it always comes down the valley," she said, "in gusts. Had you noticed?"

"No," he said.

"Listen," she said, "you'll hear it again soon. And then you'll feel it on your face. You see? Now you no longer feel it."

"No, I don't any more."

"It's gone. Wait. It'll soon come again."

They waited. The wind did not come.

"I don't hear anything," he said.

"Wait."

But they waited and did not hear anything.

"That's funny," she said.

Still they did not hear the sound of the wind preceding its advent down the valley.

"That's very strange," she said again.

"Give it time," he said.

"But I've always heard it come regularly," she said. "I've always listened to it. How perverse!"

"No more perverse than other things," he said, "but you smell nice."

"We've been sitting here for more than half an hour," she said, "and you tell me now that I smell nice."

"It's my senility showing itself again."

"Darling," she said, "why do you insist on saying you're old?"

"I'm twenty-eight," he said, "eight years older than you are."

"I don't complain. Well, not too much anyhow. Or do I?"

Eddie had laughed when he had said to him, "If it isn't an inferiority complex, then what?"

"Maybe it's your constipation," Eddie had said. Stephenson's constipation was a standing joke between them.

A noise like the snap of a dry twig made him turn round now. A man stood above them on the slope near the road lighting a cigarette. Stephenson saw him go down the slope on the left and disappear behind a clump of bush.

Thea sat up.

"I'm afraid."

Then she added, "I can't hear him. What on earth can he be doing?"

"Spying. Or easing himself."

"Suppose he's mad?"

She was smoking quickly. From the valley floor one of the parked cars moved and left a hanging line of dust over the white road. Its lights were still off. A voice called. The first man answered and they heard him come out from the bush. Thea tensed against him. He was apprehensive too. But the two men moved on.

Stephenson relaxed again. He was comfortable, very comfortable, between her warmth on his chest now and that of the ground under his back. He was so comfortable that he could have fallen asleep.

"I guess it will always be like this," he had told Eddie. "Always restless, always dissatisfied, hovering on the fringe of things, avoiding the centre or the depths. Confused, too, and wondering, and forever envious of people like you." Eddie was embarrassed. His laughter could not conceal his embarrassment.

"People who have achieved something."

"Cho man," Eddie had said, "stop it."

"Where are you?" Thea asked him now.

"Right here," he said.

"You know," she had often said to him, "you don't need me. You don't need me at all. You can do without me. It makes me feel quite useless sometimes."

"I need you, Thea."

"You're happy or unhappy without me."

"Unhappy, yes. Very unhappy."

"You sound so solemn." She laughed as if embarrassed by what she had just said.

"It's true though."

"I wish I could believe that. Sometimes I think you don't need anybody."

"It's my protection."

But because he laughed saying this she had never seemed to believe him.

"As if you need any!"

Often Stephenson was sorry for the pride with which even while she was complaining, she made the last statement. He felt quite hypocritical listening to her.

"I don't believe you do. You'll never convince me."

Sometimes she told him, "I want to get right under your skin. It's the only place I feel I can ever get close to you."

He'd laugh and say something or other and both Thea and himself would laugh at his joke.

"You're very quiet," she said now.

"I'm very very peaceful."

"And happy?"

"Uh huh."

"You'd still be happy if I were not here. I can see you lying here alone in the moonlight and being perfectly happy. All by yourself."

"It's a mistake to think so."

"Is that true? Do I help? Are you happy now, partly at least, because of me?"

"Entirely because of you," he lied.

"Kiss me." Her cigarette was a brief arc of red before it disappeared down the slope.

She clung to him. When she released him he was looking at her and smiling.

"You're laughing at me."

He put his arms around her.

"Hold me tight."

His hands, around her neck, moved.

"No, no. Hold me. Don't let me go."

She took her head away from his shoulder and lay it against his chest. She slowly removed his hands that had encircled her.

"I'm demanding," she said. "I'm sorry."

And immediately afterwards, "No. I'm not sorry at all."

And then, "Yes. Yes, I am."

Stephenson looked at the cluster of lights twinkling on the distant high hill. He could see them over her shoulder.

"You say nothing. You don't even scold."

"Why should I?"

"Don't you even want to reassure me?"

"I don't know what to say."

"Tell me I'm stupid, that I'm imagining things. That you love me."

"You know I do."

"Tell me," she said, "make me feel I belong to you."

He did not tell her what he felt about people belonging to one another.

He said, "Do I have to? Don't you know it?"

She grabbed his shirt. "Do I know it?" She was

laughing and crying now. "Oh, darling, don't you know you must make me feel it?"

He said nothing. But he was passing his hands over her hair.

"You're really old. Old for nothing. Tell me," she had thrown her head back to look at him in the moonlight, "have you ever had a girl friend?"

Suddenly it was dark. They looked up. A black cloud covered nearly all of the sky.

"We must go before it rains."

They began to walk back. Once, before the cloud lifted and the moon shone again, they heard a sudden shriek. She grasped his hand tightly. But it was only from one of the inmates of the lunatic asylum ahead of them. Every now and then, quite unexpectedly, a shriek like the one they had just heard rang out from it.

2

Two years before, after he had been on campus for only a few weeks, Stephenson had realized that he should not have come to the University College. He watched the young men who had come up with him. He imagined the sense they must have of the beginning of something important in their lives. For some there would be added to the pleasure and excitement a faint surprise that they had arrived here. A few would take it for granted, might even have wished to be elsewhere. For some it was the chance of preparing to make money if they had grown up without it, to make more if they already knew it. For all, certainly, there was the excitement and the pleasure of change. The campus was pleasant and beautiful. But for Stephenson it had merely been a change in the direction of the tide he was floating on. From his room he looked out at his mates like a rat on the piece of driftwood he had scampered on to. He had been afraid even to dip his wet bedraggled muzzle in the water that swept him, relatively safe, along with it. If he had any feeling, it was not of excitement, but of terror, a vague terror that made him very unwilling to go back again into the water that surrounded him. The young men talked and laughed, went down, as yet in their island groups, every night to the Students' Union to participate in the activities organized for their reception. They seemed to enjoy being ragged. He told himself that eight years ago he would have been as excited and enthusiastic as they were.

Stephenson had spent nearly all of the first two weeks in his room. In the late afternoon when the sun had gone down he walked to the river valley and the hill on the other side of its dried bed. He had not yet discovered the swimming pool. Sometimes he returned too late for supper. He drank coffee which he made on Eddie's percolator and smoked cigarettes. He liked Eddie. Eddie was friendly and had been helpful without being intrusive. He was surprised, and pleased, when Eddie knocked one evening on his door and came in with Val. They had returned from the Queen of the Freshettes Competition at the Students' Union.

"You missed something," Eddie said. He presented Val. Val, like Stephenson, was a freshman. He was nearly thirty, had taught for nearly eight years.

"What're you doing?" Stephenson asked.

"Mathematics. And you?"

"I don't know yet. I haven't decided."

"Val plays the organ for the biggest Methodist Church in the capital," Eddie said.

"Listen to him!" Val said. "Why didn't you come to the Union?" he asked Stephenson.

He tended to be fat, moved his hands nervously and accepted a cigarette from Stephenson. Eddie did not smoke but he invited them next door to his room for coffee. They talked about the queen who was just elected.

"She's a peach," Val said, kissing his fingers, his eyes twinkling.

"Her name's Thea," Eddie said.

After a while they talked about a musical pantomime which Val wished to put on the stage for Christmas. In the publication to guide new students, under "Societies", Stephenson had seen Eddie's name more than once. Eddie was President of the Dramatic Society, the French Club, and secretary to the Literary Society. He was doing postgraduate work in French. Stephenson drank his coffee and listened to Val and Eddie talk.

"It will clash with the traditional Christmas play," Eddie said, "and we've been reading for that since last term."

"Maybe we could combine them."

Val was enthusiastic and eager. Stephenson listened to them.

"We could put Thea Marsh in it," Val said, making a joke.

Stephenson listened to them. He had nothing to say, had vague notions only of what a musical pantomime was. Both Eddie and Val impressed him, made him envious. He had not felt like this for two years. He got up from his chair. Eddie was only twenty-one years old.

"I'll leave you to your discussion," he said.

"Right," Eddie said.

"See you again, man."

They did not even look at him. He went back to his room and lay on the bed. He thought of Ronald.

"What you doing, man?" Ronald used to say often that second year Stephenson was on the island. "It's

27

time you did something, you know." And Ronald would slap him playfully on the back.

Stephenson heard clearly the slight defect, the result of Ronald's false teeth, as Ronald spoke. He saw again the twinkling eyes in the black face, the heavy moustache over the thick upper lip.

"You gotta do something you know, boy. You can't remain like this all the rest of your life." He smiled and his gold teeth showed.

He was in England now, eating his dinners.

"Those youngsters," he used to say to Stephenson speaking of the four young men, fresh from school, who had come with Stephenson to teach on the island. Stephenson, too, had found their antics trying most of the time. He would have been very much alone if Ronald had not befriended him. Ronald took him to his home. That first year Laura had not yet gone back to their own island. While Ronald and Stephenson drank Gordon's Gin with orange, Laura sat and sewed or knitted, talking only infrequently. Mantovani was playing the Classics on a record. Laura was part white and part South American Indian. She was very beautiful and her speech was not always grammatically correct.

And it was through Ronald that he had met Rosa.

"Oh, Ronald," Edith, Rosa's elder sister, had said, clapping her thin brown hands and smiling beneath the broad forehead from which the hair was brushed back. Rosa smiled with her lips closed, her long black hair gathered on the top of her handsome head.

"Stranger," she said. She lisped slightly and spoke with a reserve that contrasted with her elder sister's buoyancy.

"I've brought a friend," Ronald said.

"I know. The new teacher," Edith smiled.

They shook hands. Edith moved around them. The dog followed her. Her sister sat on the sofa talking little, smiling but seldom showing her teeth. Her full face, a shade or two darker than the sharp face of her sister, creased attractively.

"You don't come to see us anymore," Edith said.

"He's busy," her sister said.

"Yes," Edith clapped her hands, moving from chair to table to chair, "Yes, busy with Doreen."

Ronald smiled.

"We're going to the country," Edith said, "to our farm. This weekend. Rosa doesn't want to go." She looked at her sister and made a mock pout. She resembled a small, petulant child.

"I'm tired," Rosa said, "I want to rest. If I go to the country I can't go to work on Monday. There's nothing in the country anyhow."

She got up. Her body was firm and full, the opposite of her sister's. She put on a hat.

"I'm going to vespers."

Ronald had told Stephenson that she suffered from a respiratory ailment resembling asthma.

"How's Rosa now?" Ronald asked Edith who was sitting on the edge of the chair he sat on.

"My sister suffers from asthma," she said to Stephenson. "Don't mind me, you know," she continued, playing with Ronald's shirt pocket, "Ronald and I are old friends, eh Ronald?"

Stephenson visited the sisters alone. He made excuses to Edith for Ronald and listened to her complaints.

"Ronald," she would say, "he's a coward. He's afraid of Laura and he's too busy with other women." Her frankness seemed quite in keeping with her restless, thin movements. Sometimes Stephenson met her in the street. She giggled and was never still. "Rosa is at home. She didn't go to work today. Go and see her."

Once he climbed the dark wooden stairs after school and found Rosa alone. Edith had gone to confession. When he was leaving, Rosa accompanied him to the door at the bottom of the dark staircase.

"How's Moira?" she asked, laughing. Stephenson was surprised. But when he stopped occasionally at the bank where she worked as a cashier, Rosa was distant and almost unfriendly.

The first time he kissed her at the bottom of the dark stairs she gasped several times and clasped him to her, her mouth open. He had been very frightened. She allowed him to uncover one of her breasts and while he kissed it she stood against the side of the corridor, gasping and holding him as if she feared he might fall.

After that she mentioned Moira more and more.

"Let's go to the beach," he said playfully one Sunday when he had stopped on his way to the sea.

"Me?"

"Yes, you. Why not?"

"Not me."

She said it with a curl of her lips which left no doubt about her disdain for girls who went to the beach on Sunday mornings with young men. Again he was surprised.

"Take Moira with you." She laughed.

Once or twice she met him on the street. She smiled

and passed on. He stopped once and she was compelled to stop too. But she stood with him only for a few seconds. He reflected that, on evenings, at the foot of the steps, it was very different.

One day he visited the sisters with Ronald. It was a public holiday and Edith, looking twenty-seven instead of her thirty-eight years, served drinks. The dog was sitting at Rosa's feet. It was difficult to believe that Rosa was thirty-six. The sisters were teasing the men, mentioning Doreen and Moira all the time. Ronald got up to pour himself another drink. The dog followed him to the table, sniffed at his legs, and pretended it was mounting one of them.

Rosa jumped up with that quick excitability that Stephenson had learnt behind the closed door downstairs in the dark, and slapped it. She ordered it into the kitchen.

"Excuse us," she said, very serious. "Suppose it was somebody else here?"

Edith laughed. "It's a good thing people don't visit us."

It had been a Saturday, he remembered, that he had met Edith in the street.

"Rosa is home."

"Sick again?"

"She's well now. Go and see her. I'm going to church." She held up a black book and giggled. "I'm going to confession. Then I'm going to see Mrs Lane."

Mrs Lane was her young married sister, married to an electrical engineer. Rosa and Edith, especially Edith, mentioned him often. He remembered that it had been raining very, very slightly, and the water running down the stem of the umbrella that rested against Edith's shoulders. Stephenson, who had been on his way to the library, went to the house. Rosa was in her room in bed. At first she pretended to resist. Then she opened her legs and clasped him to her. He left the marks of his shoes all over the white sheet.

And the next time Edith saw him alone she winked at him and smiled.

3

Remembering his episode with Rosa, Stephenson thought how characteristic it was of his existence and his attitude to life during the two years he had spent on her island. It was as if nothing at all mattered to him. He had come here to work. He worked and he was paid for the work he did. It was not difficult work, required no thought, no preparation. It offered no prospects either. Nor gave any satisfaction. He did not care. He was like a man on his annual holiday, in a strange land, unknown.

He had discovered, early, the beach on Sunday mornings. Remembering those mornings, Stephenson had the sensation of space without end, of a sea and a sky without any limits to them. It seemed also there were no limits to the pleasures he derived from his body nor to the increasing efficiency and strength with which it performed what he asked of it. He stayed under water for ever longer and longer periods, swam always farther and farther. Then, on his back, he looked through half-closed eyes at the hot, unending sky. He exulted in the water that was all around him, the unending line of the beach that looked, from where he was, like a thin line on the sea's edge; he exulted in the sun, its heat, and in its light. In his memory the light of those Sunday mornings dominated all else. It came off the surface of the blue water to make him squint, reddened the backs of his eyes when he was in the water on his back, burnt his face. It came off the road, too, and poured down from the sky. It seemed as limitless as his life had seemed at the time, as pure as his life was pure of thoughts about past or future.

It was different from the light on the beach of his own island. At home there were trees on the edge of the beach and it was enclosed between headlands which controlled the waves and interfered with the light. But on the island where he taught, the beach was a curved ribbon of black sand backed by no trees and stretching for miles and miles. The ends of black ribbon merged with the horizon and the waves came in uninhibitedly from the ocean. Berthed by them, up and down as he floated on his back, he felt in complete harmony with their free, uncontrolled nature. He had a sensation of well-being, unqualified, as though he were immortal or a God. He abandoned himself to a present that seemed to stretch, like the beach, forever under the sun. And it was as if this confidence in the feel and the power of his body had replaced the other confidence left shattered behind him on his island home.

He saved nothing of his salary. He paid a half of it for his board and his lodging, sent a quarter to Mémé and his mother, spent the rest on himself. He drank and listened to music with Ronald, read sometimes, visited Rosa. And he saw Moira. Like the man on his annual holiday a great part of his enjoyment was because he

34

felt he had deserved it. Life was a holiday. He was finished with thinking. The lid of his thinking mechanism had snapped shut. It was to remain shut until Carlton and Thea provided the signal that would open it again.

And so the first year of his stay on the island passed, almost unnoticed, spread out over his visits to Edith amd Rosa, his clandestine affair with Rosa, Ronald, the beach, and his affair with Moira. He was like a scorched cat, its eyes half-closed, looking at the reflection of itself and of the fire that had burned it. Life could only be an illusion, a reflection that was hedged, in time as well as in all else, by the frame that enclosed the glass. It ended when he turned away from it.

Often he remembered Moira's lamb's eyes and the quiet smile so much like that of a moron or an imbecile. Moira seemed too weary to care any more for the props other people used for support. Her eyes were without bitterness, her smile without harshness or ambition, her manner without secrecy or pretence. None of those things could matter now to her. She looked with her lamb's eyes, gave her frank little laugh, said hardly anything. And all the time her excellent body waited. Her father locked her out sometimes so that she had to sleep at the bottom of the steps in the narrow corridor. Her friends did not speak to her now or else spoke to her in the streets briefly and in other friends' houses but not in their own. And the young men, many of whom knew that body, introduced her very early to their friends, young men from other islands, who wished to be entertained. Moira seemed not to care, not even to be aware. She laughed, said nothing, and her body waited. She, too, was floating on her back and the current took her where it willed.

Stephenson had never even tried to find out what combination of circumstances had placed her there. Once she mentioned a story about a young man whom he had played cricket against, the son of one of the better-placed families on the island, now abroad studying something or the other. Stephenson was not interested. The cause, whatever it was, must have long ceased to be important to everybody. Perhaps even to Moira herself. She told him about that first abortion calmly as if she were talking about pranks she had played at the school she had had to leave. She had been sixteen and in Form Five.

He had met Moira one day walking along the flat, hot road, without any shade whatever, of tree or of building, from the beach. She was alone and walking slowly. Her flared skirt stood away from her thighs. He noticed, walking behind her, that she stood every now and then as though to rest. He came up to her and asked whether she was sick. She smiled and said she was not, not really. They walked together on their shadows along the bare road. He was hungry and perspiring freely. Now and then he felt the sting of salt in his eyes. The light and the heat was all around them. Once she stooped and wiped a leg with a handkerchief.

"You're bleeding!"

"Yes, a little."

She smiled. Her canines were sharp and pointed. There were beads of perspiration on the make-up on her face. She bent to wipe a leg every now and then.

The next day after school he called to see her. He

was not sure that she was in bed, had no reason to think but that she had merely been unprepared for her period when he had walked with her. He met her parents. Neither of them spoke very much to him and none of the occupants of the house spoke to one another in his presence. Moira told him afterwards that she had had an abortion shortly before he had met her that Sunday and that when he had visited her on Monday afternoon her parents had found out and were quarrelling with her about it. She was in bed for a week and Stephenson, who had known nothing of this at the time, did not visit her again. But when she recovered she came to see him at his hotel and brought a gift, a paper-knife with the island's crest on its head.

It had not taken him long to realize that her life, like his, was uncluttered by any hope or fear for the future, that whatever she was reacting to had found its anaesthesia in this lamb-like acceptance, this docility that opposed neither the anger of her parents nor the indifference of friends. Moira was, in fact, what he might have become if he had been forced to remain on his own island and had found a job. There were girls like Moira on his own island too and he knew that for them, as it had been for him, there was only one solution—to get out. Get out and hope that nothing had preceded you to the place you were going to.

Moira worked as a salesgirl in one of the Lebanese stores. She paid her mother for her board and her lodging, sewed her own clothes, did her own laundry. But, although it was the men who paid for the abortions, she could not save enough to be able to move away from her island home for many, many years to come.

It was a sympathy for Moira, the excellence of her body, her skill at making love, and an affinity which he felt they shared that had continued to attract him to her. He did not defend her, could not hope to defend her against Rosa's scorn even at the same time that he preferred Moira's candour to Rosa's duplicity. There was in this attraction something of fascination for that which he had so very nearly been. It was like looking at himself in the troubled waters of her own life and seeing in her calm face the wrinkled one that was his reflection and that could have been, perhaps, the original that now looked at it.

So he had merely laughed when Rosa asked with that smile on her beautiful, hypocritical face, "How's Moira?" and reminded himself, with an ugly, satisfied inner feeling, that his association with Moira did not prevent her gasps at the foot of the stairs nor her convulsive clutchings when, occasionally, in Edith's absence, he made love to Rosa.

And it had been Moira it hurt him most to leave. Rosa had made him feel a little used. Her distress, real or assumed, hidden as usual behind her little smile, left him, therefore, unmoved, gave him, even, a perverse pleasure. She would have to wait patiently for the next stranger, hoping he would not talk, unwilling to yield to any man on the island unless he married her or convinced her he would not talk. She would walk the streets, her beautiful head held high, her mincing gait as affected as her speech and, beneath it all, her fear of what might happen if she gave in to a man covered by her smile.

But Moira had only laughed when he had said he

was leaving the island, her canines sharp on the edge of her laughter, like an animal's, her eyes docile, and her ever waiting body soft and full and beginning, already, to spread just a little.

4

One day, before Laura left, Stephenson went to Ronald's home and met her alone. She complained to him. She must have been suffering much to have done so, she who had so rarely spoken to him because of her shyness.

Did he know that Ronald was divorcing her? After more than ten years of marriage? He was telling everybody she was going back because of her health. But, if she was sick, it was he who was making her, had made her so. And it was Ronald who was forcing her to go back to their island. She had got nothing out of their marriage, not even children. Maybe children might have helped. She was crying. You couldn't say it was her fault, could you? It could be Ronald's too. But one of the things he was telling her these days was that she could not have children and he wanted children. As if any doctor had said that she was responsible.

"I didn' mind working for Ronald at first. He was studyin'. All right. I could understand that. After all I'm human being. And he was studyin' not for himself alone but for me too and for our children. So I didn' mind."

But Ronald was still studying and they had no children and, in the meantime, she was getting old. He was B.A. now, but he wasn't satisfied. He had studied for five years for it while she remained at home. And when she thought she could enjoy a little now he was studying again. It was LL.B. now. And God only knew what next.

"And you know the hurtful thing is that I musn' complain."

She didn't have a home, never had one. That room she was talking to Stephenson in now, that room, here on this island, in Trinidad, in St Lucia, and in all the other places where Ronald had worked for a year or two, had always been her home. But now he was going to England she couldn't join him in a home there. She wouldn't have minded going to England, nobody would. But Ronald was sending her home. He didn't have use for her any more.

"So now I must go. You tink is fair?"

She didn't know what she was going to do.

"Look at me. You tink anybody'd look at me now?"

But there was a noise at the door and Laura disappeared into the bedroom before Ronald came in.

The day before she left there was a big farewell party for her. Edith and Rosa were among the many people present. They wished that when Laura came back it would be as the wife, not of the assistant Headmaster any longer, but of the Crown Attorney. And they looked significantly at Ronald. All said they wanted Laura to get well quickly and come back to be among them again. Edith said it too, giggling and very, very animated. But sitting briefly next to him at some stage of the party Rosa had whispered without disturbing her handsome face, "You men!"

He saw even more of Ronald after Laura had left and Ronald moved into the hotel to a room across the hall from his. Rosa never came to the hotel but Edith visited Ronald sometimes, taking care to remain in the hall and not enter his room. He and Ronald drank a lot, on Sunday afternoons particularly, and listened to music.

One Sunday, after he had returned from the beach and had looked into Ronald's room, they were standing on the verandah of the hotel looking across the street at the elderly Lebanese couple sitting on rocking-chairs on their verandah above the store. Ronald and Stephenson had their drinks with them.

"You see, boy?" Ronald said, slapping his back, "you see what money can do? You wasting your time. You know he came here with his suit on his back and nothing else?"

Stephenson was tired after the beach and his long walk in the heat. The air was hot even in the shade of the verandah. Below them the pitched street was white with heat. In the distance, along the street, the heat rose in hazy waves. The asphalt was soft in parts and showed tyre marks where cars had passed. He only smiled. His gin and orange and the ice in it was refreshing, making him even more hungry.

"And what you doing?" Ronald asked. "Teaching arrogant Lebanese boys who don't even greet you on the street."

He was smiling. He was happy. He had done a good morning's work at his Law.

Willie, big and black, and built like a mango with a cashew nut for a head, waddled on to the verandah to join them. He, too, lived in the hotel. He was a lawyer and as lascivious as any man on the island.

"Eh, Willie," Ronald said, "I was asking Stephenson what he was doing. These people came here and made all the money."

Willie laughed his good-natured laugh.

"And what you doing here, if you not making money?" he asked Ronald. "Where's the drink, Ronald, man?"

Ronald told him and he went into Ronald's room for it.

"These people," he laughed when he had come back, "know how to make money."

"Who's richer, you or they?" Ronald asked him.

Willie laughed loudly, good-humouredly. He had estates planted in lime and cocoa all over the island.

"Willie used to go to school barefeet," Ronald told Stephenson.

Willie laughed his loud, pleasant laughter. "Sometimes I didn't get to school at all."

But Stephenson was like a freed slave. Or like a wild horse riding again over open plains. He would be saddled no longer by thoughts of ambition and a fragile future. His gambols over the vastness of the present pleased him.

It had been Ronald's insistence, not any desire of Stephenson's, that had made him agree, finally, to Ronald's suggestion.

"Have you seen this?" Ronald had asked him.

"No."

It was an invitation for applicants for scholarships to the University College.

"I'm not interested."

"It costs nothing. You have nothing to lose."

"I'm too old anyhow."

But in the end he had filled in a form. Bursaries were available even for people of his age. He tried to study again then gave it up. But he sat the examination and was surprised that he should have been awarded a bursary. It was next to nothing of course but he had been awarded it. At his interview the interviewer explained that it was the college's policy to get as many people into it as possible, regardless of age. He also said that for obvious reasons the smaller islands were a little favoured in the choice of candidates. Already nearly all scholarship candidates came from the bigger islands where teaching facilities were better and methods more improved. It confirmed Stephenson's belief that he had not deserved his place.

But, as he told Ronald who was now definitely leaving for England in August, he could not accept it.

"I have no money."

"I'll talk with the Headmaster."

The Headmaster talked to Government officials. They would grant a loan in return for three years' service after graduation. There would, however, be no interest.

"Had to fight for it, too," the Headmaster said. "They said you were not from this island." He too, was not a native of the island.

But Stephenson hesitated for a long time. He began to feel that the current was taking hold again, that he was becoming more and more unable to get away from its drift. He was losing the feeling of independence and authority he enjoyed on his back, berthed by the waves, and looking through half-closed eyes at the sun. His holiday, too soon, was coming to an end.

"You want to be like Combie?" Ronald asked.

Combie was thirty-five, had been teaching since he was twenty. Every now and again he sat an examination. And every now and again he failed. Stephenson and the young men who came with him to teach earned only slightly less than Combie. Stephenson had agreed to accept the loan.

And had found out, too, soon after his arrival at the college, that he had made a mistake. His course had not interested him. He did not want to study English, had not even chosen to study it. The subjects he had studied at secondary school, the limited number of subjects he could study at college, the quantity of his loan had combined to give him three subjects to choose from: English, History, Latin. He wrote them down on pieces of paper, wrote down the numbers one to three on three other pieces of paper and drew. In that way he did not have to study History or Latin.

The need to be organized again troubled him. It was worse that he could not throw himself into the study of the language with any enthusiasm. It did not help him either that he could not think of anything that he wished to do when he left college with a degree in English Literature. He did not wish to teach, and certainly, now, he would not work in the Service either. There seemed little else he could do. Studying English was very different from studying Law as he had planned, long ago it seemed now, to do. You were not independent when you studied English. And you made much less money. In the second term he went to his professor to say that he wished to leave the college. They sat on easy chairs in the air-conditioned office. The old European listened to him. At one point in their conversation he asked Stephenson, "Do you wish to go back to teach, without a degree?"

It was the same question that Ronald had asked him.
"No," he said, "my teaching was only an accident."
"An accident?"
"Yes, an accident."
"What are you going to do?"
Stephenson had thought little of what he would do or where he might do it.
"I don't know," he said.

He could not go back to his island and he was unwilling to return to the one he had left to come here. But he did not know where he was going to. It was perhaps in order to avoid having to look at this uncertainty and indirection that he had not looked at anything other than the recurring present on the island where he had been teaching. He realized that never to look beyond the present had been his way of preserving the confidence he had re-found on the beach of black sand. To look at the blankness that was in front of him was to have his confidence shattered again as it had been once before on his island home shortly before he left it. And so when he went to Moira's he had kept his head down. It was up now and, already, he was uncomfortable and insecure.

"What then?"
"I suppose I shall have to go away."
It was a decision he must have taken but of which he was unaware until the moment he expressed it.

"Where to?" the professor asked.

"I don't know. Away."

"You've been away, been away twice. Now you want to go away again. Where do you want to go?"

He had not asked himself that question for years. Once he had known he was going to England to become a lawyer. It seemed he had clung to that dream so improbable now.

"I suppose I could go to England."

A plan, it seemed, was forming as he spoke to the professor, vague and imprecise as that plan yet seemed.

But the professor, smiling still, asked him, "And after England, Mr Stephenson, and after where you'll get to after England? And then, after that?"

They had talked some more and the professor had stood up.

"Perhaps you'd like to think some more about it?" he suggested. "And we can talk about it again near the end of term, yes?"

Stephenson went out into the brighter light and the natural heat on the verandah. Two days later he had met Carlton who had come to cover the talks on the federation of the islands. The college had offered a building for the talks. The road leading to it was lined with flags and crests of the participating territories. Every night there were meetings between students and their islands' representatives at the talks. Students discussed the proposed federation seriously or in fun. Groups of students, for and against, were formed, held talks themselves, gave demonstrations outside the Conference Hall. The campus was full of reporters and visitors.

Carlton was talkative and confident. He knew all about politics, local and international. He had spoken to all the leaders and leading politicians of all the islands, knew exactly what everyone thought. The talks would break down, he was sure of that. His buoyancy depressed Stephenson. Carlton seemed to hold all the answers in his fine waving brown hands. The islands were not ready for federation. The Home Government was only anxious to get rid of the islands. The local leaders were greedy and selfish. Listening to him, Stephenson, completely uninterested in politics, was dazzled and depressed. Carlton, his brown hands never still, talked and talked.

"Let's go for a drink, man," he said, "or you going to lectures or what?"

His accent was like that of the people of the large island in the south where he worked. Looking at him Stephenson saw little of the young boy he had grown up with on their island home. Only the brashness now remained, exaggerated and, Stephenson found, a little depressing.

"Go back?" Carlton said when they were drinking beer in the Students' Union. "Me? Go back? Back to what? Or to where?" His hands, never still, opened wide with the final question.

"You think I could go back to work for ——?" and he mentioned the island's only newspaper. "Not even if they made me editor." He waved his fine-fingered hands. "Those boys have nothing to offer me, now."

He told Stephenson what his salary in the larger island was.

"Right," he said. "You think they'd want to pay me

that at home?" He sucked his teeth, gave a little laugh, patted Stephenson on the back.

"No, sir," he said, "I aint going back. Old Carlton is all right where he is."

It was perhaps then that Stephenson thought he was sure he had glimpsed the insecurity that lurked in the shadow of Carlton's brash assertiveness. Carlton could not go home again now, even if he admitted that he wanted to, except on holiday or after he had retired. He had joined that ever growing list of young men who left the island and went elsewhere to work and could not return because the island could not cater to them. They were exiles forever. Unless in the meantime he went beyond his school certificate to a degree, won a sweepstake, or, Stephenson thought, became a politician. He listened to Carlton for a long time. They drank much beer and he became more and more depressed.

And that week, for the first time, he asked Thea to go out with him. She agreed.

5

He had been meeting Thea at the pool on many mornings, had noticed that, when she smiled, her lower canines were as sharp and pointed as Moira's. But her eyes bristled with life. There was nothing docile about Thea's eyes.

Stephenson had seen her very many times since he had heard Val and Eddie talk about her in Eddie's room. The pantomime, directed by Eddie, had been a success. Val's music was much praised, on and off campus. There were favourable reviews in all the newspapers.

Stephenson, who had agreed to manage the curtain for Eddie, had seen the play at rehearsals and every time it was performed. Sometimes he and Thea exchanged words. It was only during the second term, when, as she said, she had more time, that Thea had begun to go to the pool.

He had listened to Eddie tease Val about Thea. After rehearsals it was Val who often walked Thea back to her Hall. Sometimes the four of them, Eddie, Thea, Val and himself, went to the Students' Union for beer. Stephenson was still thinking seriously about leaving the college. He looked upon everything that he did in it as part merely of a very, very short interlude. He thought of himself as a sleepwalker; and of Thea, Val, and even Eddie, as figments of a dream he would soon awake from. Thea, therefore, seemed particularly inaccessible, more inaccessible even than her relationship with Val, as it seemed at the time to Stephenson (she was to say later in the pool that Val and herself had only been friends), alone, would have made her seem.

Thea attracted him. The country girls whom he and Carl had tumbled on the hills of his island home, the partners of his temporary alliances when he was working in the Customs, the whores and the women on the fringes during his last two years on his island; Rosa, Moira—none of them had prepared him for Thea. It is possible that, whatever he saw that was strange in her, it was he who had invested her with it. But he made her seem, or she was, different from any woman he had come close to before. There was of the country girls in her; she could throw back her head and laugh loudly. There was in her of Moira; she seemed without any airs whatever, natural and unaffected. And there was in her something he associated with girls at home, on his island, going to school in the Convent, whom he had looked at and never spoken to. She resembled Rosa in her complexion and in the build of her body, and in nothing else. He felt she would never have slapped a dog trying to mount his heels. She would have laughed at it.

He did not ask her to go out with him until his meeting with Carlton had added to the doubts his meeting with the professor had raised for him. Carlton had frightened him badly. Stephenson had decided that a degree, in anything, once it served to protect him from Carlton's insecurity and the brashness which Carlton needed to cover it with, was preferable to this blankness he saw when he lifted his eyes to look, in time, ahead of him.

He was preparing, then, to go to collect Thea the evening they were going out together for the first time when the porter said that there was a lady at the porter's lodge to see him. He thought Thea had come to say she could no longer go out with him. He went to the porter's lodge. He did not recognize the fat woman standing before the door of her car, her lower lip trembling, her hand, the black handbag hanging from the forearm, against her abdomen.

"You don't remember me."

It was Marie Desportes. He had not seen her for several years, had never been a friend of her's. Once, when Mémé was sick, Dr Desportes had come to the house to visit her.

"I should never have recognized you," he said, when they were sitting in his room. It was after six and against the rules that Marie should be in his room, but nobody checked very seriously. He saw that Marie had been crying and did not know what to say.

"I had to come."

She took out a packet of cigarettes from her handbag and Stephenson lit both their cigarettes.

"I'm in trouble."

She told him about her divorce that was pending. Her husband had come to the house on the school grounds, had called her all sorts of names, accused her of all sorts of things. They had fought. In the end it was the Headmaster who had had to intervene. She'd been so ashamed.

"Excuse me," she said, "I know it's not pleasant. But I heard you were here and I had to talk to somebody."

She could not go to Phyllis and Peter. They were in the same boat as she was. Did Stephenson know that? Of course, he would, everybody knew about Phyllis and Peter. Anyhow she could not go to them. And she did not trust the people of this island, no matter how friendly they pretended to be. She knew them, her husband was one of them. Stephenson listened and thought of Thea.

"Would you like some coffee?"

She nodded. She was crying again.

"Excuse me."

He went to the telephone. He told Thea he was sorry he would have to be late and promised to explain when he saw her. Then he went into Eddie's room for the electric hot plate and the percolator.

Marie remained for more than two hours. Stephenson gave up thinking about Thea, imagining all the things that could happen when he saw her. They drank much coffee and smoked cigarettes. When Eddie returned from the library Stephenson called to him and Eddie joined them in a cup of coffee. Stephenson introduced the two. While Eddie was in the room Marie spoke of her experiences in America where she had gone to university. Stephenson remembered that Dr Desportes had a brother in America and that it was in the United States that, at forty, he had qualified as a doctor.

They called Marie's father Dr Quack after a notorious doctor in a cheap American film, and "Prescription Doctor" because, they said, all he did was look at you and prescribe patent medicines. They said he had an understanding with the drug store where he had worked as a dispenser before he went away to study.

Dr Desportes had married again when he returned from America. But he had not married the woman with whom he had lived after the death of his childless first wife and who had borne his two children. He married Marie's mother. She forbade her stepdaughters to enter the house on the edge of Columbus Square, would not allow her only daughter and child to talk to her stepsisters. The doctor had to be content with seeing his older children in his office or during his visits, more and more infrequent, to their mother's home.

People said of Marie's mother, "Never see, come see, come crazy." They said that she did all she did because she was the first black wife to live so close to Columbus Square.

After a while Eddie left and said he had some work to do.

Marie had heard of what had happened to Stephenson at home.

"I was so glad to hear you were here."

He had only been unlucky. She knew that everybody was doing *Bobol*.

"Anyhow, it's past and over with. And you're here now."

How were Phyllis and Peter? Did he go often to see them?

"Dr Peter Breville," she said, as if she were feeling the phrase.

"Who would have thought it?"

She told Stephenson, what he had already said he knew, of the fights and quarrels between Peter and his wife, of Peter's drinking and chasing other women, of Phyllis's jealousy and determination.

"But what did you expect? After all . . ." she did not finish the phrase.

Where were Phyllis's brothers now? One never knew, did one? Imagine . . . ! They had not wanted Peter for Phyllis because he was too black. Now . . . ! Who could tell? She had heard that one, Johnny, had gone to Curaçao to work in the oil refinery, but she had no news of the other. Did Stephenson know?

Stephenson said that he did not know, but four years ago when he was just about to run away from their island he had heard that Dunstan, the brother Marie did not know about, had emigrated to England.

class

"He couldn't be more than a bus conductor now," Marie said.

She was happier talking about Phyllis and her family. Was it true that the mother had another child, after fifteen years? A black one?

Stephenson said it was true.

"Imagine that."

Marie shook her head and smoked.

"A black child. After all that fuss. If only we could tell the future!"

Stephenson smiled. He answered her question about the big house old Desmangues had acquired for Phyllis's mother and the children on the other side of the market. Stephenson knew the district well. He had lived quite close to it.

"Big house or not," Marie said, "it was still where the prostitutes lived and the porters and the sellers of fried-fish-and-bread."

She sucked her teeth. Stephenson told her the house was derelict, the roof uncovered in some places, that nobody lived there any more.

"They thought it would never end." She smoked and sipped her coffee. She seemed already to have forgotten why she had come to Stephenson in the first place.

"I didn't like Phyllis at school. She thought she was too this and that."

She talked about Phyllis's pretensions when they were at school together.

"But she was only an illegitimate child, even though her father was white."

Stephenson smiled. Marie saw it.

"I don't mean you," she waved a fat hand, "you're not in that."

"Of course."

"You're half-white and illegitimate, too. You don't mind my saying so, I know. But it is not the same thing at all. You know that."

"Yes, I know. My father was not an estate owner."

"Exactly. And you didn't put on airs."

"I couldn't afford to. I had no airs to put on."

She continued to talk and Stephenson began to think of Thea again. He wondered what she would say to him when he went so late to her with this absurd story as an excuse. It could only happen to me, he thought. And he wanted to laugh.

"Anyway it's Peter's fault, too. He liked white skin."

Stephenson seemed to have just entered, as if he had not been hearing the almost uninterrupted flow of Marie's monologue.

"He had no time for black girls like us. Serves him right."

Marie laughed and lit another cigarette. Stephenson suddenly wondered at the intimacy that had sprung up between the two of them after just two hours in his room on this island. He had not spoken to her three times before. He remembered her serving tea with the other convent girls to the schoolboy players the year the inter-island schools tournament took place on his island. By then, Phyllis had already left school, forced to do so by the death of her father. Stephenson had learnt from conversations between Mémé and her clients that the house they lived in was the only thing Phyllis's mother possessed. The legitimate heirs of old Desmangues had given them nothing else.

He had become very friendly, too, with Peter and Phyllis. Yet, at home, he had known very little about either of them. Peter had left school at the end of Stephenson's second year, had disappeared soon afterwards. It was an old story.

In the Customs, sometimes, he had listened to stories of boys and girls, men and women now, and his predecessors at secondary school. Nearly all the girls were on the island. Only a very few, like Phyllis or Marie, had been able or willing to leave it. They worked in the Civil Service or, if they were of the right complexion, in banks and travel agencies. Many of them were spinsters and, like Rosa, though perhaps without her extreme duplicity, many had clandestine affairs.

But nearly all the boys he heard of had disappeared from the island. They might all be dead. "Knobby",

"Skippy", "Bones", "Coeur Campeche (Hardwood Heart)", were names only to him.

"They've nothing to stay here for," Mr Jones, Chief Executive Officer, used to say. He was forty-nine. married, had five children. He said he did not know how he would take care of them.

"I should have gone, too, I'd be better off. A hundred times better off."

He touched the epaulettes of his Customs Officer's uniform nervously. He drank and smoked too much and had a slight cough. He was always talking about cricket.

One day, shortly before his arrest, Stephenson met Ernest in the streets, carrying a child on his shoulders. They had been in the same class until Ernest had had to leave school because he had made a young elementary school teacher pregnant. He had had to marry her in order that she might not lose her job. He found some work as an overseer on one of the estates in the centre of the island. After two years his wife had died and the second child with her. Ernest looked haggard, was drably dressed. He had been aggressive at school and precocious with the convent girls. Of his class, Stephenson realized, he and Ernest were the only two who were left. Clive was becoming a priest. Selwyn had gone to relatives in Trinidad, many had gone to the oil refineries in Aruba and Curaçao, David . . . they had all gone.

"They all go," Mr Jones used to say. "And you? Aren't you planning to go too? No solidity, no continuity. Every year a little pocket of one or two boys remains. The others go. Some, most of them, never come back. There's nothing before for those who stay to build upon. They'll leave nothing behind for others to build on. And that's how it is. I'd want my children to go away too."

While Marie talked and talked, Stephenson thought of Mr Jones, of Ernest, of the Knobbys and the Skippys. And he thought of himself, of Ronald, who was from another island. And he remembered Carlton. He told Marie, when she was sipping her coffee, that he had met Carlton only a few days ago.

"He left yesterday after the conference was over."

Marie asked how it felt to be about to belong to a nation. Stephenson said he did not know, had not thought about it at all.

"Another form of partisanship," he said, "another reason for intolerance and bigotry."

"I'm thrilled," Marie said.

He told her Carlton had prophesied that the talks were going to break down.

"But the results of the talks proved him wrong."

"Carlton's always a talker."

"A lot of people are not too happy though."

"Yes. Especially those from this island. Those . . . !" She did not say it.

"They think they too big," she said instead.

They talked still. About other people and some events on their island. Marie had not been home, she said, in ages.

"I'd like to go back though," she said.

When finally she rose to go, she had completely recovered from her depression.

"You must come and see Sheila before they take her away from me."

Sheila was her eight-year-old daughter. She gave Stephenson this verbal invitation with a smile.

6

Thea's middle-class background, not, like Marie's, newly acquired, but handed down for at least three generations, contrasted with, made him aware of his own parentage when he was with her. He listened to her stories about her grandparents and her great-grandparents and kept the story of his own forebears to himself alone. He did not know his father, had not lived with his mother, had nothing in common with his brother, Carl. He did not remember what his grandparents had looked like, would have had no stories to relate anyhow to Thea.

"You never speak about your parents."

"There's nothing to tell. We're from the country. I'm just a country boy trying to make it."

They had been going together now for nearly a year. The first academic year had ended, he had told the professor he was staying. Thea had gone to spend the holidays with her uncle. Mr Marsh had only recently been transferred to his new job as Crown Attorney on the other, smaller, island. Stephenson remained on campus, but he did go to spend a weekend with Peter and Jeannine in the mountains in the Great House which had been a gift to the university. Jeannine was

French and an assistant lecturer. Stephenson had understood that he was being used by Peter to lull Phyllis's suspicions. He and Peter left alone but waited in one of the small bars along the road to wait for Jeannine to join them.

It was cold and sunless even in the foothills. Half an hour after they had parked the cars and begun to climb the steep, narrow track behind the donkey, the house appeared through the mist and a dog ran onto the damp lawn in front of it barking and wagging its tail. The cateress came out. She had prepared tea. They sat on the verandah in their sweaters and looked at the mist outside. You could see nothing beyond it. Stephenson wished Thea were there with him. The boards of the old house creaked when they walked. The cold on his face was pleasant. He had never felt cold like this before.

He left Peter and Jeannine alone, saw them at meals and at night when they all sat before the fireplace sipping rum and water. He walked alone along the tracks, saw nobody, looked at the mountains when they showed, sometimes, through the mist. He wrote all that he did and saw that was strange to Thea; but every time he discovered something—a flower, the mist on the mountain-top, the pleasant, infrequent sun after the cold—he said to himself, "I wish Thea were here to enjoy this."

The second academic year began. He and Thea were a "campus couple" now. Together they went to the pool on mornings, walked, on afternoons, in the river bed, along the road, between it and the playing fields, to the small village the cooks and the janitors came from.

Sometimes they climbed among the stunted trees of the hill on the far side of the dried river. Evenings, they walked over the wide lawns of the campus. They made love, too, now.

She made him laugh again, had made him from the very first. He realized how long it had been since he laughed, really laughed, laughed as he had not laughed since he had lost the job in the Customs, as he had laughed as a boy with Mémé, or in the hills with Carl and the girls on moonlit nights.

Sometimes, on mornings after she had left him alone in the pool to go to her lectures, he thought of himself and Thea, years later, married, having children. He saw their home, the kind they would be able to afford, and he felt an anticipatory satisfaction for their children who would never have to wait as he had had to.

For the second time in his life he saw the future opening before him, taking shape, having firm roots already in the present. And, too, as it had been that first time, it was so real that, already, he was living it. He saw himself looking back with wonder, from some point in that so already certain future, at the young man he had been. From that imagined but secure point he looked back at himself, swimming now in the pool, already surprised at the many turnings of his short life of twenty-eight years. Like a snail it had never overcome any obstacle: it had always and simply moved around it. He had tortured a snail once, in the yard behind Mémé's house when he was a boy. Every time the creature wished to move he touched its antennae with a stick. The creature withdrew them, veered, pushed them out again, tried to continue. Stephenson touched them again. He touched their sensitive rounded tips every time the creature tried to move. Finally the animal withdrew them altogether, went inside its shell, and was still. Stephenson waited. The snail showed an antenna tentatively. Stephenson touched it. The animal withdrew it again and disappeared. Stephenson waited then for a long time. Finally, disgusted, he turned the animal on to the back of its shell and went away. He had very nearly crushed the shell to make it come out. Four years ago (already it was four years) he had been like the snail: in its shell and refusing to come out. But now his antennae were out again.

He would lie in the pool with his thoughts. He was in the present but it was a present that included the remembered and the imagined times of past and future. He was ready to take up his snail's advance where it had been disturbed. There was no break in the line; no break between the past he remembered and the present and future he was in now. His whole life, its continuity, seemed to be resolved in his relationship with Thea. As if, all along, and in spite of everything, it was to her that he had always been heading.

And it was for this reason that he was afraid. There were areas of his past life he would have to explain. And he did not think he knew how, or that he wanted to explain all, or any part of them, to Thea.

But the second academic year ended, too, and Thea went away for the holidays again, this time to her island. Stephenson spent the vacation working as a secretary to the Drama Course of the Summer School. Now the year had begun and they were together again.

Stephenson awoke and sat up on his bed. The sound

of cups and saucers from the dining hall must have awakened him. He had overslept. He lit a cigarette and dressed while he warmed some coffee. From one of the blocks a radiogram was playing a calypso loudly. Someone shouted. It reminded him of the mad shriek he and Thea had heard the night before. From other students there were shouted protests against that loud sustained shriek. It was repeated. Someone laughed loudly. Another swore. A door banged. Stephenson sipped his coffee.

He was afraid to have to explain his past to Thea, afraid, too, to let her see how much she meant to him.

"You must keep your secrets very well," she had said last night.

"I have no secrets."

No secrets indeed! His very need of her he kept a secret, away from her. As though, thereby, to keep it from himself as well; as though he was resolved never again to know that he needed something so greatly that its loss might shatter him.

He heard the silence as the thermostatically-controlled cold store from the kitchen shut off. It was its hum, to which he had grown accustomed, that he had not been hearing. From the other block, loud voices accompanied the radiogram.

"You know, you don't need me. You don't need me at all. Sometimes I think you don't need anybody."

"It's my protection."

And she had never, never believed him.

With a click the cold store in the kitchen began to hum again. He heard it then ceased to hear it any more.

The telephone on his block rang. After a while he went to answer it. The call was for him, from Marie. She wanted to come to the dance the college was holding the next Saturday.

PART TWO

7

Marie stopped humming the tune the band was playing and, smiling, said, "I'm having a very good time, you know. I'm glad you asked me to come."

"Good," Stephenson said.

"Even though it was I who invited myself in the first place."

They laughed.

"I like Eddie. He's nice."

"Eddie's all right."

"Doesn't look like a postgraduate student at all. Looks more like a freshman."

"He's very young. And very bright."

"I haven't been to a dance in years," she said.

"In years?"

"Well . . . it's been such a long time."

She smiled. Then she asked, "How old is Thea?"

"Nineteen."

"Take care of her."

Stephenson smiled and did not answer.

"We like to be taken care of," she said, "especially when we are young. But you should know that. You're old enough."

Stephenson smiled and said nothing.

"Would you believe I was like Thea once?"

"No," he laughed, "you're too fat."

"Used to dance well too, like her."

"You still do."

She laughed. "Thanks," she said, "but I can't move now. Not with these hips."

"You look like a Spaniard dancing with your hands on your hips."

"The first big, black Spanish dancer I ever saw," she laughed. "You're full of compliments."

She looked at the dancing students.

"Look at them," she said. "I used to be as happy as they."

Then she said, "I wonder if they're all as foolish as I was."

"Why do you say that?"

"Once I thought I should have been happy for life," she smiled at him. "I wondered how all people were not happy. How people could quarrel and be vindictive. How marriages ever broke up."

She sipped her beer. He lit a cigarette for himself and, at her request, one for her.

"You're breaking your resolution," he said.

She smiled through the smoke.

"I've broken many resolutions," she said. "Without noticing, I broke my resolution to be happy. How many resolutions I must have broken since only Heaven knows! Let's dance."

They climbed onto the crowded dance floor.

"Your Roman Catholic friend must be sleeping by now," he said, "while you're enjoying yourself."

"It was really she who insisted. I think she wants to

go to Holy Communion tomorrow. She's not like you, you see. She's a true Roman Catholic."

"I'm not a Roman Catholic."

"You are."

"I was."

"Once a Roman Catholic, always a Roman Catholic."

After a while she said, "And she's so young. It's a shame."

"She's married again to God," he jeered.

"Isn't it silly? Married, in this day and age, at twenty-six and not knowing a man before. I believe her too."

"No man before, and now no man after marriage," he said.

"It's no joke."

"It's not not a joke either. You think she'll last?"

"She seems very sure of herself."

"Time," he said, "will tell."

"Time always does, doesn't it?"

"Oh yes."

"How many people must have wished Time had told sooner."

"You don't know the story then?"

"What story?"

"The story of the aged youth."

"No. Tell me."

"He wanted wisdom without age. God gave him the body of a baby and the wrinkled face of an old man."

"Which God?" she asked him.

"There always is a God," he said, "there must be. Or didn't you know?"

"I thought there wasn't for some people."

"Anyhow God, his God, gave him the youngest body and the oldest-looking face."

"A monster," she said.

"People flock, nevertheless, to see him. They watch him smoke cigars with his soft pudgy hands. They watch his hairy legs bend and curl, like a baby's when he's on his back, and they listen to his words of wisdom through the cigar smoke. Then they go away and forget him."

"I could never forget him," she said, laughing, "could you?"

"Oh," he said, "that's the whole point. You have no choice. It's his punishment to be forgotten as soon as he is out of sight. He can never share his secret with anybody else. As soon as they leave him they must forget all the learned sayings they heard."

"What a weight", she said, "for him to bear."

"Yes. What a weight."

"Much heavier than I am."

"Much much heavier."

They laughed.

"Let's sit," she said.

They walked over the wet grass to their table. She sat at once. He wiped the dew off his chair with a handkerchief. The two other chairs were upside down on the grass.

"I always forget to wipe the chair," she said.

"Nobody will notice now, anyway," he laughed.

"I'm tired," she said, "and amused. Thanks."

He bowed. Then he said, "It must soon be intermission. The band's been playing for a long time."

"I hate intermissions."

"Why?"

"The noise. Everybody talks, everybody laughs, everybody walks about, goes to the toilet, waves to friends."

"The sound of happy humanity. Eddie might say that."

"Everybody's wet and sticky and complaining of the heat. Yes, and everybody's happy."

"And tired."

"And tired. And eager for the dance to begin again."

"We're not tired here," he said.

"I wasn't tired too. But I'm tired now."

They smoked a cigarette.

"The holidays are coming again," he said.

"The holidays have just ended," she said, "and I'm tired already. No. I'm still tired."

"Take your car. Go for a drive." He waved his hand holding the cigarette, a wand in the moonlight conjuring voyages to nowhere.

"Where to?" she asked.

"Anywhere. To the mountains. Make a tour of the island."

"I'd have to come back," she said. "In any case I can't go alone."

"And your friends?"

"They have their friends."

"Even the Roman Catholic? She, at least, should be free."

"She'd make me feel inadequate as well as tired. She's too well organized."

"Then become a nun," he said.

They laughed.

"I think, sometimes, she's a lucky woman."

"Do you now?" There was banter in the voice.

"She has stability and equilibrium. Her religion's like a lifebelt around her neck."

"Around her waist, too," he said, "like another belt in the Middle Ages." He and Marie, no friends on their island home, had been drawn by their expatriation here, on this one, very close to each other. "And sometimes, around her eyes, like a band."

"You don't think it's good for her?"

"It's like false teeth. Only an appearance. To eat with it is hell."

"But life is not an endurance test. We need those things. Or don't we?"

"It's easier."

"We're not heroes."

"Nor always puppets."

"We need help to cope."

"The old story," he said.

"What story?"

"The story of the crutch and the limb."

"Oh? I don't know it."

"The limb atrophies, the crutch becomes ever more necessary."

"You're strong," she said, "most of us aren't."

"I'm not strong. I'm only a mangy dog. I've learnt to be wary."

"I know."

"If more of us were . . ."

"I'd hate to think of casualties," she said, "we are not all alike."

"Casualties," he said, holding up the word to the moon. "A meaningless word in our time."

"I thought it was I who was depressed."

He smiled.

"I'm lonely," she said. "I'm one of the casualties."

"A fat, prosperous-looking one."

"I want a man, a companion. I'm getting old. I don't want to live alone, grow old alone. It shows too, I think."

She told him of the young teacher at her school who had tried to kiss her on his second visit to her house.

"I was annoyed. He said he saw I was lonely. I didn't know it showed so much."

"You look very self-contained to me."

"I thought I did. I try to."

"But there are those we cannot fool. Those looking for victims and those who wish to understand. We can escape neither."

"He was definitely looking for a victim."

"Who knows?"

She grunted.

"Anyway," he said, "you're young. No more than thirty."

She smiled and refused to confirm what he said.

"But I'm alone," she said, "and tired of it. And of other things as well. Every month I get more tired."

She sipped her drink.

"I went to see Sheila today," she said. She's owing nearly a term's fees and the nuns say she'll have to go home if they're not paid. I don't know what's wrong with the father. And Sheila herself is so backward. I don't know what will become of her."

She dabbed at her eyes with her handkerchief.

"That man's a wicked man, I tell you, a wicked

man. And now he's married again and me . . . look at me."

She dabbed her eyes again and smiled suddenly at him in the moonlight.

"Cheers," she said, "I am behaving like a little girl."

"Cheers," he said.

"Go home," he said. "Go back home to our little island. Get married again there."

She looked at him.

"You must know I can't go back," she said.

"Why not?"

"I can never go back," she said. "I have to stay here with Sheila."

"With Sheila? To see her only once a month on visiting day at school?"

"Well for Sheila, if you like. But I must stay here. I cannot go back. At least not for a long, long time."

Stephenson remembered Carlton and his slender, brown hands that were never still. Carlton had stated his inability to go home again aggressively. He had sought to hide the pain of his enforced exile. Marie, now, owned up to it quietly, with resigned regret. And every step that he had been taking in recent years had been leading him, Stephenson, farther and farther away from their island home. He wondered, seriously for the first time, whether he would ever go back to it.

"Have you told Thea?" Marie asked after a while.

"No. Not yet, I haven't."

'You're going to marry her?"

"I don't know," he smiled.

"She's nice. I like her. But she's young, remember that. You should tell her."

"I expect I shall."

"Tell her before someone else does. Tell her, then marry her."

He smiled.

"I know," she smiled as well. "That I, of all people, should tell you to get married! But it is what you should do."

The long session of calypso music came to an end.

"The drinks," he said. "It will soon be impossible to get near the bar."

He left hurriedly for the drinks. Eddie and Thea were sitting at the table when he returned. Thea was fanning herself, as if she did not want to, and sipping from her glass. She leaned forward to place the glass on the table and Stephenson saw the patch of wet on her back where she had perspired.

"Had a good time?" he asked Eddie.

"Yes. It was good, wasn't it, Thea?"

"I'd do it all over again," she said.

Marie laughed, throwing back her head. "Aren't you tired?" she asked.

Thea shook her head.

"No," she smiled, "I think I could go on dancing all night."

"I'm sorry I should be unable to oblige," Eddie said, "I'm beat."

Stephenson had finished opening the bottles of beer. Eddie served Marie. Thea held her glass out to Stephenson. The scent of her perfume rose to his face. The noise of simultaneous conversations rose all around them. A glass or bottle fell on the concrete floor and shattered. Heads, including theirs, turned then turned again. They sat back in their chairs unwilling, now, to make the effort of conversation against the noise. People cast brief shadows on their table and on themselves as they passed. The moon came off the wet grass and the empty bottles at their feet. Beyond the lawn, on the road, the tops of parked cars reflected it. The uppermost leaves of the trees behind the cars played with it and with the dew that had collected on them. Thea and Marie threw stoles over their shoulders. Thea and Stephenson looked at each other across the moonlight and smiled. After a while the band struck up again. People clapped their hands and turned to look at the bandsmen. Above the noise from the tables one, two, three instruments were heard running through the musical scale. Soon the band was playing. Thea and Stephenson danced.

"Dr Breville," Thea said in his hair.

He swung her around and saw Peter in a hot shirt dancing, slightly drunk, with Jeannine. She was looking up into his face and smiling.

"He's making a break by Jeannine," Thea said.

"I hadn't noticed."

"You don't see anything do you, darling?"

"I suppose not."

"Are you having a good time?"

"Yes."

"Good," she said, "I am."

Then, "Don't drink too much please."

He said nothing.

"I'm not complaining. It's not a complaint. But heavy drinking's not good for you, darling. It makes you weak in bed."

He smiled. The music stopped. He began to move towards the table. She restrained him with the barely perceptible pressure on the hand she still held. The music began and they danced again.

"Why was she crying?" Thea asked.

"How did you know she was crying?"

"I don't know. I wasn't even sure. I just felt she had been."

"She's not happy."

"Oh."

"It's about her child and her ex-husband."

"Hush. I don't want to hear. Let's talk about something else, please, darling."

"There's something I must tell you," he said.

"What is it?" she asked. What he felt of tenseness as he held her would have sufficed without the sharpness of the tone of her voice.

"Something I should have told you before."

"About us?"

"About me."

He felt her relax.

"What is it?"

"I'll tell you later."

Peter and Jeannine danced close by.

"Hello, you two," Peter said.

"Hi, Peter."

"'Night, Dr Breville."

"Call me Peter, Miss Marsh."

"My name's Thea," she said.

"*On s'amuse?*" Jeannine asked Stephenson.

"*Oui.*"

They danced away.

"He's mad," Thea said.

"He must not be very good in bed."

"How do you know?"

"He drinks, as you would say, too much."

He felt her face move against his neck as she smiled.

"*Touché*," she said.

The music stopped. They stood waiting.

"Do you want to go back?"

"Do you?"

"If you do," she said.

"I want to do what you want," he said.

"I don't want you to stay if you don't want to."

The music began again. They danced very well together. They made love, too, Stephenson reflected, very well together. Their conversation while they waited for the band to start playing again, its carefulness, its mock consideration, made him remember them sitting on the grass in the middle of the wide lawn.

The next morning he had gone back and stood looking at the cigarette ends and the half-burnt matchsticks strewn over the ground. Only a few hours before, Thea and himself had sat there, smoking those cigarettes, talking and finding it more and more difficult to find a dry spot to sit on. They had sat and talked until two in the morning. Wet bits of cut grass clung to their clothes and to the palms of their hands when they placed them on the ground for support.

At one stage, smoking furiously, Thea had said, "It didn't matter. It was you I was thinking of all the time."

At another stage, he could not remember whether it was before or afterwards, "But don't you see? I didn't have to tell you. I could have kept quiet and you'd never have known. But I told you. I wanted to tell you. I knew I could tell you and that you'd understand. You must understand. You have to."

Outside her hall she had asked, "Are we still going to the dance on Saturday?"

"We have to. Marie and Eddie are coming with us."

She had nodded.

"Goodnight."

"Goodnight."

After she had gone he talked some time with the conniving porter. He took half a packet of Haynes' cheap island-made cigarettes, for he had smoked all of his and most of hers, and paid Haynes for a full packet. The porter had pretended to remonstrate.

"Cho man, Mr Stephenson, me no like dat."

"I'll get them back some other time."

"De same way you'll get the games o' draff dem from me? Is how much you owe me now, suh?"

As he stepped down into the night, Stephenson had wondered if he would be continuing much longer to play draughts with Haynes while he waited for Thea to come down from her room to him.

Now on the concrete floor, the music having stopped, they were returning to their table.

"Did you see Peter?" he asked Marie.

"No, I didn't."

She was in the process of sitting down and still panting from the last dance. Eddie, courteously slender, stood behind her chair, helping her.

"Any change?" she asked Stephenson.

"He drinks more than ever."

"Poor Phyllis," she said, "even though I never did

like her at school. I wonder what her parents have to say now. Phyllis always had a head of her own, always knew what she wanted."

"She's got it now all right," he said.

"Is she here too?"

"What do you think?"

"Who's it this time?" Marie asked.

"One of us."

"A student?"

"No. She lectures in the Modern Language Department."

"Stephenson's friend," Thea said.

"Peter's overdoing it," Marie said, "after all the child's dead."

"What child?" Thea asked. "Not Dorothy?"

"Oh no."

"No," Stephenson explained, "not Dorothy. Their first child. They were married because Phyllis was expecting it."

"Oh."

"She got him anyway," Marie said.

Stephenson laughed. "You don't have to say it like that."

"That's how she meant it, I can tell you. Whether she was almost white and he was black. Whether her parents objected or not. She wanted him and she did what she did to get him. And now she has him."

"I'd hate to be an enemy of yours," he said.

"I have nothing against her now. But that's what's happened. So why try to hide it."

"Nobody's trying to hide it."

"Anyhow why doesn't she get a divorce?"

"And do what? Go back to her parents? What parents?"

"Her mother, anyhow."

"She's better off where she is. And she knows it. She doesn't want a divorce."

"She has guts. I must give her that."

"She probably loves him, too," Thea said.

"That's a dirty word," Marie said.

"Sounds like she's in a trap," Eddie said for the first time.

"If it's a trap, she loves it. She says he is doing what he does so she may divorce him. Well if that's what he thinks he'll see. She'll never divorce him, she says."

"Her marriage is all that she has now, really," Thea said.

"It's not much is it?" Eddie said.

"But she must hold on," Thea said, "I don't see any alternative."

"It's a hell of a price to pay," Marie said.

"What a depressing conversation," Thea said.

"You're absolutely right, Thea," Marie said, smiling.

They talked of other things in the moonlight. It came out that Eddie was a very good footballer.

"You play football then?" Marie asked him.

Eddie would not answer.

"He plays," Thea said.

"Very well, too," Stephenson said, "he plays for the college and he has been playing in trials for the island's team."

"All right," Eddie said.

"Congratulations," Marie said.

Thea took a cigarette and lit it. Stephenson watched

the fall of moonlight on her long neck as she put back her head and exhaled smoke. After a while they left Eddie alone.

"I believe I owe you an apology, Thea," Marie said some time later.

"Whatever for?"

"You'll never guess," Marie smiled. Her liking for Thea came out with her smile and with the tone of her voice. Perhaps, too, the liking for the girl she used to be. Thea waited.

"Do you remember the first time you went out with Stephenson?"

"Oh, it was you!"

"Did he tell you what I made him listen to that night to make him so late with you?"

"No," Thea lied, smiling, "he didn't."

"I hope he never does," Marie smiled. "It would only depress you."

"I never shall," said Stephenson.

The bottles of beer were all empty. Eddie got up for some more.

"Anyhow," Thea said, "it ended very well. We went for a walk. We walked to town and back."

"A long walk," Marie said. "Enjoy it?"

"Oh yes. But I was tired."

"You're too young to be tired," Marie said.

"Funny too."

"Oh yes?"

"Have you ever walked down High Street after eight?"

"Not in the night, no."

"It's completely empty. We had the entire street to

fool in. Once he climbed a traffic policeman's dais and was directing me. You should have seen him."

"Stephenson?"

"Yes, Stephenson."

"I don't believe it."

"And don't you ever believe it," Stephenson said.

"But it's true," Thea said, "he made me laugh the entire night."

"You make me sound like a frustrated clown," Stephenson said, "but everybody knows the truth."

"What's the truth?" Marie asked him as Eddie arrived with the drinks.

"I am a clown," Stephenson said.

"True," Eddie said, and began to open the bottles of beer.

"We were very happy that night," Thea said.

"Let's be happy now, Thea," Eddie said. "Let's dance."

Stephenson and Marie followed them to the dance floor.

"You must take care of that girl," Marie said. They were dancing without holding each other. Her hands were on her hips. Her dress hung from them as from hoops.

"Oh," she said, "there's Mr Small. I didn't know he was here."

Stephenson, when he had exchanged places with her, saw a tall man with a bow tie and a white jacket.

"He's our headmaster."

"I know."

"Of course."

"I love him," she said.

He said nothing. They danced.

"I love that man," she said.

Stephenson said nothing.

"That's his wife dancing with him. Did you know that too?"

"No," he said.

"I still love him." she said.

"Love is a dirty word," he mocked.

They laughed.

Then he said, "I know all about it."

"Naturally. I've just told you."

"No. I know all about it, everything."

He reminded her of the night of her party when they had decided it was too late for her to take him to the campus and then drive back home alone. From the hot guest-room he had seen Mr Small walk along the corridor before it which led to her bedroom. He had seen him in the light that came in through the glass window.

"I keep that light for burglars," she said. "So you saw him!"

"Uh huh."

"And you never said a word."

"Why should I have?"

She laughed. Suddenly she caught herself laughing too loudly and put a hand to her mouth.

"I wonder how many of us fool ourselves like that?" she said.

He said nothing.

"I was sure I was careful, that nobody knew."

"Obviously you were not."

"It's stupid, isn't it?"

"You certainly didn't fool everybody."

"I wonder if I fooled anybody?"

"Maybe some."

"Or was I fooling only myself? I could not have fooled the young man who tried to kiss me."

"No. I don't think you did."

They danced around each other.

"I've been a useless hypocrite," she said.

He said nothing.

"I couldn't do even that properly."

She took her handkerchief from the bosom of her dress and dabbed her eyes.

"I've made a hash of everything," she said.

"Do you want to stop?" he asked. "Do you want us to go and sit down?"

"No," she said, "I want to dance."

They continued to dance.

The music stopped. They moved towards their table. The dance was nearly over.

Marie said, "Bring Thea to the house some time. One Sunday. We can have souse."

"Okay," he said.

"I'll come and collect you. But make it soon. The rains will soon start."

"I'll let you know."

"Eddie too."

"Of course."

Some time after the dance was over they stood, except Eddie who was more comfortable now if he sat, around her car waiting for the other cars to move off. The two women, their stoles over their shoulders, were chatting. Stephenson spoke to Eddie through the car window. Then Marie left with a final wave of her hand to drop Eddie, first, at the Hall of Residence and then drive home, alone. Thea and Stephenson began to walk. They walked down the hill to the playing fields. The noises of cars ceased. Their shoes on the asphalt were the only sounds. Moonlight glinted on the wet grass on either side of the road which turned several times and descended steeply. On a similar night, and after a dance too, he had kicked his heels over the wet lawn on the way to his room, swinging his arms and smiling at himself under the moon.

"This is not me," he had denied. "I cannot be so happy." And then still skipping along he had asked this question of himself, "What have I done to deserve such happiness?" There had been no one to put the question to, nor to share in the happiness that impelled him like a child over the grass. The Halls of Residence were in shadow behind their moon-washed verandahs. But he had heard the flushing of a toilet and when he turned towards the hills there had been the cluster of lights flickering dimly because of the moon and the mist on the distant high hill.

"It's beautiful," Thea said now.

She gasped. They had come to the end of the hill and the playing fields were spread out before them. The pavilion stood out of them like a doll's house, the moon on its roof. Its open interior was in shadow.

"It's like a field of frost," she said. "Let's walk on the grass."

"You'll ruin your shoes."

"I don't care about my shoes."

She walked over the grass making little noises of

pleasure. On the other side of the road, behind the swimming-pool, the walls of the changing-rooms were in shadow: but the wide concrete ledge around it carried light up to the feet of their dark wooden sides. Their galvanized roofs reflected it. She joined him again. She sneezed twice. They heard the sounds taper off in the night, chasing each other. She took his arm.

"Now," she said, "I've caught a cold. But don't say anything, darling. I feel like being foolish tonight."

Later she asked. "Is it the moon that makes me feel so strange?"

"Perhaps," he said.

"Everything looks so unreal. I feel a little unreal myself. Are you real?" she asked, and laughed in his face.

The day after their long argument on the wet grass they had walked after dinner to the open bit of lawn in front of the lecture rooms across the road from the library. The building was ablaze with light. Inside, the silhouettes of heads and shoulders showed. They were still talking under the tree when, at nine o'clock, the lights went out and the library was closed.

"We were pretending," he had said, "both of us. Now we can continue the pretence or we can stop."

The surprise and the hurt of the previous night had already disappeared. After he had gone to bed he had looked at himself and Margaret, in August, sitting together on the same bare patch of hill below the road looking at the sunrise over the river valley and lying naked in his single bed, hot and uncomfortable, every night during the final week of the Drama course.

There had been a dance and presentations the last night. The secretary of the course had also received a gift. Margaret made the presentation to him on behalf of the class.

"I'm leaving early tomorrow," Margaret had said later. "It's a long drive back to the north."

"Will you write?"

"I wouldn't like Thea to find my letters when she comes back from holidays."

He had not known that Margaret knew about Thea.

"What do you want to do?" Thea asked now.

"To stop seems logical," he said.

"Can't we continue?"

"We can always continue if you like."

"If I like. And what about you?"

"I don't think I know," he lied. "People normally stop."

"We are not people. Don't you feel anything?"

"No," he lied again.

"I don't want to stop," she said.

They had walked to the Students' Union afterwards for beer and cigarettes. They had answered the gibes of their friends with the same old laughter and their usual bantering tone.

Now Thea and Stephenson had left the road and were walking over the damp path to the pavilion.

"It's like an arena," she said. "The lions will come out at any moment."

The moon was white on the grass below them. Soon they were in each other's arms. He made love brutally to her, both of them fully dressed on the narrow bench at the back of the pavilion. They were talking about it, she questioning and he trying not to answer, when a car descended the hill and drove on to the fields below them. Its lights went out, the sound of its engine stopped. It might have been deposited there, now that the night was quiet again, by a fairy or by a god. One of its doors opened and Peter came out.

"It's Dr Breville," Thea said.

They watched him walk over to the other door, open it and pull out a woman. Stephenson recognized Phyllis. They watched the man and his wife fight.

"He'll kill her," Thea said, as the woman picked herself from the ground for the first time. "Oh God. Stop them before he kills her."

Once again the wife picked herself up from the ground. From the shadow of their raised position they watched the woman fall a third time in the moonlight and support herself on one arm. They heard her crying quite loudly now. Stephenson had the feeling of unreality that Thea had mentioned to him earlier. He watched Peter pick up his wife, unprotesting and without fight, and put her in the back seat of the car. He went inside and the car disappeared behind the hill. They saw it again appearing and disappearing as it climbed.

"My God," Thea said. "Oh my God."

8

That night Stephenson told Thea of his arrest and his trial. They had put him in a cell in the police station and kept him there for two days.

When he had told her, earlier at the dance, "I have something to tell you," he had done so on an impulse only, perhaps pricked by the conflict of Marie's well-meant importunities and his own thoughts. He had forgotten his promise. It was her insistent questioning of his manner of making love to her on the pavilion bench and the prospect, on the grass arena before them, of Peter and Phyllis, that had reminded him of it again. He discovered that he could not tell her of his arrest alone. Even if she had not repeatedly interrupted to ask, "Why?" he would have needed to go back a step behind each action or phase of the life he was describing to her. In this way he was retracing, like a traveller going back along the line of imprints of his feet in sand, the events he had lived. It seemed, as he related them, that no single part of the recital was complete without what preceded or followed it. And so, after a while, he broke off his disjointed, interrupted and backward-moving narrative and began instead from the beginning.

His father, he told her, had been a sailor. In those

days the island was still a coaling station and he used to watch the women climb and descend huge planks leading from the wharf to the ships' sides loading and unloading the coal. Ships came regularly into the harbour for coal and water. His mother, lent by her parents from the country, went sometimes, sent by her guardian, to join the other women behind stalls on the wharf selling jams and other local products. Tourist Boards had not yet taken over and selling local produce was still an individual affair. You made the things and sold them: or you bought them from those who made them and had no time themselves to go to the wharf. Rosanie, his mother, was only eighteen when he was born.

Her parents and her guardian had been friends for a long time. There was no question of blame or quarrel over her conception. For years his grandparents had been supplying charcoal and vegetables and eggs weekly to their friend in town. They had grown up together on the hills of the infertile north before Lucita left for the capital to become a servant to a mulatto seamstress. After many years she had bought a second-hand sewing machine from her mistress, a small machine, worked by hand, and had rented the small wooden house she had ever since lived in. When her friends were in town the house was their house. They ate and rested there.

Lucita had not married, had no children; and Stephenson and his mother lived with her until he was three. Then Rosanie moved back to the rainless hills to live with Marc, her new husband. Soon it was they who came most often to the town. Marc brought charcoal on his donkey, a bag on either side, as many as three times a week sometimes. When he had finished selling the coal he took Stephenson for rides on the back of the animal to tether it near the blacksmith's on the edge of the town where the road led to the hills. He collected it on his way home.

Once yearly the seamstress put her machine aside, closed the small wooden house and went with Stephenson to spend a week in the country. It was Easter. Because of the amount of sewing for women who hoped to wear their new dresses on Good Friday and Easter Sunday and Monday, Mémé was unable to leave until quite late on Maundy Thursday. Marc waited with the donkey. Then Stephen climbed the animal and sat behind their baggage. Later, on the high road, Mémé took her turn. They lit the lantern when it was dark and Stephenson carried it with pleasure. After about three hours they left the road and climbed wide dirt paths. The house stood high on large stones and a short wooden stair led to the door. The others came out with lamps to meet them. The dog barked. He fell asleep on the wooden floor while the others were still talking.

In the morning, early, he sat in the doorway, his legs hanging over the edge of the floor, drinking coffee and eating stale bread and arrowroot porridge. In later years his brother, Carl, five years younger, joined him. There were hills everywhere. Smoke rose from charcoal pits he could not see here and there. It was only later he realized why there were no villages and the houses were so far from one another. There were no valleys here, for sugar-cane, and the hills were neither high enough nor wide enough for clouds to drop much rain. There were no estates here.

Every year he spent holidays in the hills. Mémé went

less and less frequently. His grandparents died. He went to the little house by himself now not for a week but in August and September for all six weeks of the holidays. He was now at secondary school. He had won a scholarship. It was during the war. In the town West Indian soldiers walked the streets. Americans were everywhere. They walked with their arms around the women. There were more women than he had ever seen before on the streets. They came from the country, too, with their hard calves and their patois. Where he lived was full of them. It used to amuse him to listen to their imitations of the speech of their American and English friends. Often there were fights between the American and English sailors: sometimes between the white sailors and the West Indian soldiers. Once a group of American negro sailors beat up a policeman with sticks until he fell. From behind the closed jalousies he and Mémé watched. She could not prevent him from watching. They beat the fallen policeman until he no longer moved. The street was empty. Everybody looked from behind closed windows. Nobody went to help. Later they took the policeman to the hospital and he went with the other boys to look at the blood on the street.

People fought and pushed for bread. The lines outside the bakeries were very long. Sometimes he went and pushed too with friends and shouted for the fun of doing so. People dried breadfruit, pounded it and made bread. You couldn't get Canadian salt cod, nor salt oxtail nor mackerel in brine. His parents brought Mémé food and crabs from the swamp far from where they lived. There was always plenty of food in the house and sometimes Mémé gave to her friends. When the war was over there was a torchlight procession to Government House on the high famous hill at the back of the town and he watched the lights moving in a line over the dark hill. Later that night they distributed free rum on the market square which was reserved for animals that were about to be slaughtered but which for years had not been used.

But because he was in the hills he missed the torpedoing of two ships in the harbour by enemy submarines in the second or third year of the war.

Carl was now much bigger and stronger than he was. He had never been to school and spoke only the patois of the island. Stephenson joined him and his father when they went to make charcoal. In the evening they returned. They walked over the steep tracks, hard underfoot (he was barefoot, too) because of the lack of rain. Around them hills arose from crevices deep as the one they seemed continually to be climbing out of. A shout sounded. Sometimes the blow of an axe. The sounds echoed. Parts of the hill were in shadow. Slowly the cloud moved. The hill was like a cat awakening. On the other side of a gorge, from another charcoal pit, smoke rose in the air. They passed men in tattered trousers and old felt hats with dirty singlets or old jackets and their cutlasses in their hands. Sometimes they carried bags of charcoal on their heads. The boys wore nothing above their torn shorts. The bigger ones carried loads almost as heavy as those of the men. Through the holes of their old frocks the slips of the women showed. They greeted one another in patois as they passed and those who happened to be descending the slope stood aside to allow the others to climb. Then the sun set. The hills were in shadow and dead trees stood white on them everywhere. Bare patches of earth, cultivated with yam or dasheen, lay between areas of stunted bush. Only on the tops of the highest of the hills to the West did the light from the sun still show.

They threw down their loads and washed their feet with as little water as possible. The breadfruit and salted fish pushed steam upwards through the leaves and the piece of cloth that covered them. Later they ate sitting on low stools in the open space before the house, the fowls coming out of their sleeping places to peck at their feet. Then the lamps were lit. The thick unchimneyed smoke disappeared into the night. They sat out in the now pleasant warmth for a little while.

Sometimes when there was a moon Carl and himself went to gatherings of young people and sang and laughed. They put their hands on the breasts of the laughing girls. Sometimes they felt pants made of coarse cloth under the thin frocks, sometimes no pants at all. Afterwards they walked home for miles through the wet leaves. Dead branches snapped under their feet. The moon was areas of light in the open. Under the trees it was white dots lying on the ground and flitting over their bodies as they passed. The girls and boys he played with, the girls especially, called him *"ti béché"*, little white man.

In the meantime he was going through secondary school, a good sportsman and a fair student. He topped his class in mathematics. He played cricket and football for his school and for his island. In its small capital people began to know him. His name, among others, appeared in the newspaper. He left school. He was seventeen, was going to become a lawyer. The world, before him, opened wide. But he joined the Civil Service like everybody else. One or two of his mates, rich, went to England or America. He went to work in the Customs. He would have to be of those who waited.

Commerce, stopped during the war, had begun again. Commodities, unobtainable before, were coming into the island now. Everybody wanted them. Contraband goods, especially wines and spirits, came regularly from Martinique. Fines were stiff. Bribes, therefore, correspondingly large. He sold cloth, rum, cigarettes, perfumes, everything. And he accepted bribes. Finally they caught him. He had bribed his way out before. He could not do so now.

When they released him two days later he went to the hills to Carl, Rosanie and her husband. He must have dreamt of Mémé's face behind the old-fashioned glasses and the way she had lifted her head from her hand-machine to look at him every night of his stay. He went back to town and his trial two weeks later. He was surprised to find that the magistrate was a former schoolmate recently returned from England. There was no sign of recognition between them. After three days he was convicted. His lawyer had pleaded extenuating circumstances, mentioning the old seamstress, and the magistrate spoke to him severely, as to someone he had never known or seen before, and fined him heavily. Between the fine and his lawyer's fees, the money he had saved over five years, all of it, was gone.

The old seamstress went at once to the church. People talked and winked their eyes over the verdict. He felt that he had been given a chance. He went back with Carl, who had remained with him during the trial, to the hills. They killed a fowl, a rare thing, in order to celebrate. His mother made the sign of the cross as the tears formed below her eyes.

He remained a month in the hills then went back to the town. Mémé's head seemed to be bending ever closer now to the needle of the machine as she sewed. There was much grey in her hair. He had had no time before to notice that she was ageing. When she saw him she said, "The Lord works in mysterious ways. We must not question nor try to understand what He does." She said it so perfectly that he knew it was a quotation she had read somewhere and memorized. He was suddenly aware of how much he had neglected her and of how much she must have been hurt, even though she did not complain, by his indifference. For years he had been coming to the house only to eat and to sleep.

He remembered now days of sitting on a little stool at Mémé's feet playing with discarded reels, matching cast-off bits of cloth he had picked up from the floor. Mémé turned the handle of the noisy machine and hummed and spoke to him.

In the weeks that followed he had plenty of time to remember. He spent long days on the beach. He became lean and hard and the colour of wet sand. He swam, slept, walked on the hot sand, read, looked at the clouds. He thought about himself. He walked in memory with Mémé on the edge of the water in the soft sand and laughed to himself at her old-fashioned bath suit.

On Christmas Eve she used to sew until nine o'clock in the night, the lamp standing on a little shelf on the partition above and to her right. People came in and out. Some came and went several times. Others sat down and waited. They gave him presents and money. Then Mémé put away her machine and baked cakes and roasted pork from his mother in an old biscuit tin placed over a coal-pot. There was the smell of baking, of meat being cooked and of the rum she used to make falernum with. The sorrel leaves fermented in the jar. When he uncovered it a sour-sweet smell arose. He ate bits of cake stuck to the bottom of pans, bits of pork, sucked a bone, sampled the sweetness of fresh ginger-beer. Often he fell asleep long before twelve. Sometimes she awakened him just before midnight to kneel and pray with her. At midnight while they prayed the bells rang out from the Protestant and Roman Catholic churches, ships in the harbour blew sirens, fireworks exploded. Then it was quiet until people returned from Roman Catholic mass. Mémé, who had been fasting, joined him in a meal of pork and bread. One or two people knocked on the closed door as they passed and said, "*Joyeux Noel*" and "*Bonne Fête*". Then the streets became quiet again. The fireworks were sporadic. He fell asleep. At other times he would awake long after dawn on Christmas Day. Mémé was up and making sorrel. She had been to midnight mass while he slept. The first minutes of the New Year they kissed and exchanged gifts of oranges. They had to keep the seeds safely throughout the year for luck.

He lay on the beach and, when he was tired of remembering, he slept. He returned to the house on evenings after dark. He ate supper and went to bed. He was tired and slept soundly until the next morning. He avoided the beach on Saturday afternoons and on Sundays and holidays.

He received an unfavourable reply, signed for the Administrator, when he applied for his old job in the Service. Then, in turn, his letters answering to advertisements in the local paper for junior staff received unfavourable replies from St Mary's College and St Joseph's Convent. He had now been going to the beach every day for three months. His one daily meal at Mémé's was like a reproach. Her uncomplaining too. His money, even that which he had given her for herself, must long have been exhausted. He began to worry. He had up to then acccpted as natural, given the circumstances, everything that had happened to him. He had not complained, had still felt he had been lucky. But now he approached managers in the bigger business houses. They shook their heads. That, too, seemed acceptable. After all he had been convicted of a charge of theft. When the managers said, "It's not my fault, I've spoken to the boss. He says no," he accepted that, too, and went back to the beach and read and looked at the sky. It was certainly logical and in the order of things. But he began to feel, lying on his back and looking at the clouds, that everything had been removed from his hands and that, from now on, he was to have very little say, even no say at all, in what happened to him. Indeed it began to seem, on reflection, that he had never had any.

He did not remember when he first began not to sleep at night and to think instead, in the dark, of how to get out of a system which, while it was perfectly normal and logical was, nevertheless, tending very really to destroy him. In any case after the first two nights he decided it might be better to go out and walk. Soon he was going to the beach during the day mostly to sleep. And at night, while other men slept, he walked.

One afternoon on the beach, after sleeping all morning, he awoke to see a woman in the water. She came out and he saw that she had the figure of a bag of charcoal on sticks. She spoke only patois. He joined her in the water. Soon her legs were around his waist and her arms about his shoulders. The water was up to his neck. She came once or twice more. They lay on the sand under the sea-grape and the coconuts. Then she did not come again. He waited a few hours that first afternoon and then forgot her. Perhaps she had got some work now to do. She had merely been another accident that happened to him.

A little later his wild dreams began. Walking past the banks late at nights he had thoughts of breaking into them and sailing to another country far away. He wondered where the safes of the business houses he passed were and how much money they contained. His wild ideas, impossible of realization, made him feel trapped. He dreamed on his feet of walking through the night and emerging into another place, another time. Mémé's uncomplaining nagged him. He didn't want to eat her food any more. He was tired of his half-brother's quiet, imperturbable concern. He was tired of people's pity and of his own that was beginning to emerge.

Sometimes, at night, he sat on a bench on Columbus Square. From the church on one side of it the clock struck the quarter hour. He looked at the clean, two-storeyed houses with electric lights, not kerosene lamps.

Cars were parked in the quiet empty streets. He heard voices on the verandah, saw the moving tips of cigarettes in the dark. Sometimes he saw people leaning over the verandahs. Their accent was different. Some of it was foreign. They were lawyers and doctors, held executive positions in the larger business houses. A few were white, none was, as yet, black. Some of the whites were the poor relations of those who lived on their estates in the middle and the south of the island. In these houses the rulers of the town lived, the members of government, elected and nominated, the professionals. They were the descendants, legitimate and illegitimate, of Europeans who had owned slaves on the island less than a hundred years ago. Their complexion, their names, the circumstances of their birth had given them an advantage. They were, now, nearly all old. But at the time he did not know that their advanced age proclaimed the end of an era. He was too preoccupied with his own problem to think about it.

Sometimes an old man with a torn jacket and gaping shoes shared a bench with him, not speaking. Stephenson learnt to wait for the young college student and his girl-friend, a teacher in one of the elementary schools. He would have liked to know what the old man's life had been, to imagine what the lives of the boy and the girl would be. Ten years ago he had been like that boy. The old man, too, once, had been as young. At ten o'clock the sirens sounded, and the women, and sometimes the children too, came out with their buckets. The little town was filled with the smell of human excreta. One or two of the women worked until the early hours of the morning. At eleven or thereabouts the people came from the cinema, first the cars, then the pedestrians. Then the night was quiet again. The young couple had long gone. The old man too. He began, then, to walk.

Sometimes he spoke to a policeman he had once played football against or once had bribed. They smoked cigarettes, the policeman taking care to hide his. In the early hours of the morning he headed for that part of the town where he lived near the market. He walked along the littered streets past the rancid smell of small shops, past the smell of fried foods, past rum-shops and the smells of urine and of vomit. He swerved to avoid little puddles of liquid on the pavements, a drunk where he had fallen, or men and women sleeping between bags under the verandahs of houses. Sometimes the occupants of the house had thrown water on the pavement to prevent the sleepers from laying their bags in front of their homes.

He learned the sounds of the night: the scrape of a piece of paper blown by the wind, the whispering of a couple just within the dark of a yard, the ticking of a clock in the house he passed before. The sights too: the quick shadow of a cat, the straggling drunk, the policeman standing in the corner or a fisherman, his bamboo mast over his shoulder, hurrying from his home on the other side of the river where the houses were even smaller than the one Stephenson lived in.

Sometimes he saw a woman walking alone. He followed her. She refused or she did not; demanded money or asked for nothing at all. It was all the same to him. Sometimes he passed a house where there was a party. Light from an open window threw a square on the pavement. He moved to the other side of the street. The voices were sometimes familiar, sometimes not so. He walked, his head down, his hands in his pockets. The sound of the gramophone and of laughter followed him. It meant nothing to him.

He was going to do something, he knew that. It could only be something "rash" now. He knew, too, what was going to happen after he had done it. His sins, as he had known, could not hide here. The island was too small. But he had no choice. Quietly, compulsorily, he was beginning to make a decision. The present had become intolerable. He had no clear idea of what he would do. He knew, had been shown, what he could not do; and that left him with possibilities only of what he could do. But each possibility, in the end, was reduced to this: he was in a stranglehold and would have to fight if he wished to escape from it. How to fight was not clear. Yet he had visions of policemen who, too, must do something in order to live, and of law courts; of eventual sleeping under verandahs at nights with friends he had met in gaol over many terms of imprisonment, of a long steady descent into rowdyism, squalor and every other kind of degradation. And he thought, too, of his ex-friend the magistrate, and of his impersonal face as he spoke down severely to him from his comfortable seat.

He had his romantic moments too, he told her, moments which allowed him the pleasure of a temporary release from the reality of the present and from the bleakness of the cul-de-sac he saw when he tried to imagine the future. He saw himself in the hills, the leader of a band of brigands similar to those who, once before, had taken to those very hills. Those slaves had been fighting for their freedom. He too, though in a different way, would be fighting for his. They had been fighting a system that had seemed no less logical than the one he saw himself, in his dreams, fighting now. They had been defeated because, being against the system, they had to be. And he too, he was sure, since he could see no way of escaping, would have been defeated as well. He might very probably have been in gaol now, now that he sat here in the pavilion telling her about it, if yet another accident had not befallen him. He read one day an advertisement for a junior master in another of the small islands and applied. The headmaster happened to be from his own island and he got the job. And that was all.

He was neither surprised nor even excited. His desperation went as quickly as it had been growing gradually. He had learnt that everything, everything, was possible. One thing only, he had decided while he walked through the nights, did not change: you were born, you lived, you died—sooner or later. He had got the job. What had happened was behind him. What was to come, ahead of him. He would meet it, whatever it was, whenever it came. No more plans. No more disappointments. No more hopes. No excitement of any kind.

Stephenson stopped. He had just told Thea another lie. It was excitement that had prompted him, when he had left her after after the dance that night in June, so much like the one just ended now, to gambol over the grass, baying his happiness like a dumb dog at the moon. He knew, now, why he had told her. He had brutalized her physically on the bench earlier, given her something physical to repudiate, to find repugnant: he was brutalizing her again, giving her himself to repudiate, find repugnant. He realized clearly now and for the first time that he had decided to leave her.

"Why have you told me all this?" she asked. "Why did you tell me—now?"

Dawn was breaking. Around them the pavilion benches were in disorder. Pieces of paper lay on the floor. He looked away from her anxious face and at the hills. The cluster of lights in the distance went out only seconds after he had turned to look at them.

"Why?" she asked again.

And then she said, "I knew it. I knew it even at the dance. Everything that happened tonight was leading to it. You're going to leave me."

He looked at her again. She seemed even more anxious and her eyes were grave and looked steadily at him.

"I suppose I must be," he said.

"I don't despise you," she said.

"Nor me you."

"I had no idea it would hurt so much."

He seemed about to speak. She went on.

"You fooled me. Your pretence took me in. I thought you were strong, self-sufficient. At least you must believe that. Forgive me."

"You understand even less than I have understood."

For it was only now, as he began to speak again, that he believed he saw more clearly.

"I, too, slept with a girl while you were away."

"It doesn't matter," she said.

"You mean now we are quits?"

She shook her head. She no longer seemed anxious.

"No. I don't think Lloyd has anything to do with it."

"I wonder how much of what you're saying is self-protecting?"

"Maybe a lot, maybe none at all. I was not aware you were a psychologist."

Her eyes were still grave. She gave a little laugh. "Your story was very dirty in parts, deliberately. You wanted to shock me. . . . Of course. You did, didn't you?"

"I think that must have been my intention all along. I only realized it when I had finished though."

"You haven't succeeded," she said, smiling again and her eyes still steady and grave. "You've numbed me. The whole night weighs like a block of ice. But," and she smiled again beneath her grave eyes, "I'm not shocked."

"I don't think I want you to go though," she said after a while.

"I don't think I want to go either."

"Then why?"

"I don't know. It seems a decision I stumbled on by accident only, not a decision I made."

They smoked a cigarette. The day had truly begun. Cooks and janitors from the village behind the playing fields were taking a short cut across them on their way to work. The swimming-pool attendant had come and the noise of the pumps reached them where they sat.

"I'd like a swim," she said.

"And bathsuits?" he asked.

"There are always other people's."

Something about the hills he was looking at again

caught his attention. Then he saw what it was. The lights had been switched on again. He was about to mention it to Thea when, abruptly, they went out. He said nothing.

The sun appeared over the hills while they were in the cold water of the pool. They swam two or three lengths then came out and sat in the sun, their legs dangling over the water. There were some male students now, members of the university swimming and water-polo teams, come to train. Stephenson and Thea exchanged jokes with those among them whom they knew well. Then the team were busy practising and Thea and Stephenson watched them. Occasionally he retreived the ball for them.

"Yesterday," Thea said, "I received a letter from home. I meant to tell you, but I forgot. It was as if I knew what was going to happen. Mummy liked your picture. Daddy too. They both approve."

Stephenson said nothing.

"You're the right complexion, you see," Thea continued. "Mummy thought you'd look nice and distinguished, her words, if you wore a beard."

"Do you know how you sound?"

"They're like that," she said, "both of them. Dull and middle-class. And quite prejudiced. Mummy's always nagging Daddy about her family and how they had silver for breakfast. Daddy, who's very handsome, has women outside which distresses Mummy even more. Mummy complained to me. She said I was old enough to understand. She said Daddy was spending so much money on women when the family needed it. I felt sorry for her but it was ugly and sordid and it wasn't my business. I didn't want to be involved. A week after I arrived home I was sorry. It was a relief to go out with Lloyd."

She shrugged her shoulders.

"They didn't like me to go out with him. He was not very fair and he was only a junior civil servant. I went out every time he asked me to."

She turned to him and smiled.

"You see," she said, "your story could not have shocked me so much. I, too, know things."

"Forgive me." It was his turn now.

She smiled still.

"I was just like an animal."

"A hurt, cornered animal," she said, "but it was I who provoked."

"What animals!" he said. "And how we need always to stand at our sides with sticks."

"And after all this," she said, "you'll still leave me."

"I suppose. There was no need to hurt first, though."

"Do you want to know something?"

"What?"

"It was very flattering once I had understood why."

He snorted.

"It was," she smiled.

"What was the name of your girl?" she asked him.

"Margaret."

"Was she pretty?"

"Not half as pretty as you are."

He told her also what Margaret had told him, that in a month's time her fiancé, who was studying dentistry in America, was coming to marry her.

They got up from the edge of the pool.

9

Eddie died the Sunday of Marie's souse and drinks party. At three that afternoon they drove from Marie's home to the stadium where Eddie had to play a football match. The rainy season had begun. There was some thunder and lightning, and the match had almost been abandoned. Shortly after the match had begun Eddie and three other players were struck by lightning and Eddie and one of them had died. From the pavilion, Stephenson, Marie and Thea had watched it all. Now at nearly twelve o'clock of the next day his parents and some friends had come to collect Eddie's belongings.

Sitting in the doorway of his room Stephenson watched them. Eddie's father was very old. His mother was young and might almost have been his sister. She had been crying; but the old man with the white hair was almost stern as he listened to the Hall warden who accompanied them. Stephenson moved away. He was unwilling to listen to their conversation or to have to tell Eddie's father that he was sorry his son had died. The heat was damp and unpleasant. It would soon be raining again. Thunder rolled distantly in the background and the lightning seemed only a harmless reflection. Somewhere the storm had already begun again.

He took his raincoat and put on his canvas shoes. The ground was soggy underfoot, the grass, green and wet. The leaves of the short hedge were green, too, and the flowers showed washed colours among the green. He walked along the corridor, past the porter's lodge and on to the road.

He had not wished to think of Eddie any more than he had wished to hear bits of his father's conversation with the warden or to say that he was sorry. But he found himself thinking of his friend's "brilliant promise and already significant achievement". He had read those words in the papers this morning. He had been envious of Eddie. Now there was nothing to envy any more.

Stephenson thought of his own pursuit of achievement which had pushed him to dishonesty and which, all along, had been the principal cause of his fear and of his dissatisfaction. He had lied in the pavilion when he told Thea that he would take whatever came, whenever it came. Beneath his pretended indifference, like the fear beneath Carlton's brashness, his frustrated desire always had milled. He asked himself now, for the first time, whether what he so much yearned for was worthwhile.

He could have been comfortably married at home, going every day to work, drinking after it, at home with friends, at their homes, or in one of the clubs, waiting for his steady slow promotion if he were in the Service, based on seniority and therefore inevitable. Sundays, sometimes, the family would go to the beach. He would attend cricket and football matches, discuss heatedly the final selection of the island's cricket and football teams. He would be glad sometimes to have a drink with some of his friends from schooldays gone abroad and returned qualified and independent. And he would pretend they did not make him envious. Perhaps, since he would have elected to stay in the first place, he would really not be envious. Neither the inevitable quarrels with his wife about other women or his too-heavy drinking would interfere with the even, contented tenor of his acceptance.

He saw himself, like Mr Jones, growing old; his children growing up, his drinking more necessary if not more enjoyable, quietly, unambitiously, and complaining, like Mr Jones too, playfully only, and because it gave him something to talk about.

Stephenson asked himself whether that vision, so clear now as he walked, was not of a way of life that was preferable to the one he had chosen or that had chosen him. He had tried to persuade himself that perhaps he was not responsible. That he could not have denied or prevented that desire for achievement that had driven him nor the dissatisfaction that not having it caused him. He had told himself that he was merely that which, ever since his birth and without his having any say at all, he had been tending to become. Now, talking actually to himself as he walked, he wondered whether it was not too simple an explanation.

He thought of Carl and Marc going in the morning before the sun to the charcoal pits and their vegetable patches, and then returning in the sunless heat of the evening to eat and sleep. They did what was there for them to do and nothing else. And they were, or seemed, content. He had not heard Carl desire anything once except, perhaps, the trousers that he was saving to buy.

He thought of his friends at home in the Service or in banks and offices earning, in comfortable acceptance, their pensions and their promotions, deriving their pleasures and satisfactions only within the perimeter of the island's affairs.

All of them seemed to him infinitely more comfortable, more peaceful in mind and spirit, more intuitively happy. And he remembered Mémé growing old alone on the island. It would have been so easy to accept and, accepting, be happy and a source of happiness as well. He felt guilty about Mémé who was soon going to die. And he, who had been envious of Eddie, envied Carl and Marc and his friends waiting to die at home.

He thought of Ronald and of Laura, the wife he had put away. He thought of Combie and his exams and of the magistrate, his schoolmate, who no longer recognized him in the court room. He remembered Dr Quack, Marie's father, now dead. These had known the side of the dividing line between the many and the few they wanted to be on. But Eddie was dead, too, even though he had always been on the right side of the line.

Stephenson snorted. It was an old story. Centuries ago, on posters, in prayers, in popular songs, death had always nipped achievement in the bud. And he had not known what the people who lived in that time so long past had already known—that human effort, in the end, if it did not benefit others, was futile. It was Ronald, he thought, even though they seemed so different, even though he thought he understood Ronald so completely, he most resembled. He suddenly felt small, futile himself, insignificant. He hunched his body even more under his raincoat.

He made a noise with his mouth. He was committed to his pursuit of futility. His original instinct, reinforced by Carlton's concealed panic, had been transmuted into a necessity that would benefit ultimately not himself but his and Thea's offspring. But he had broken with Thea, was looking to no future with her or their children. He was alone again, working to benefit no one but himself. Mémé would die soon. There was little he could do for Rosanie and Marc or for Carl. But he could not stop. To stop now would be to become, for everyone, mad. For himself, to stop would be falling again into the paralysis of his fear of the future, bemired in an ever continuing present. Even the snail in Mémé's yard had not been able to stay in its shell forever. It had already moved when he came back to look for it. As Marie had said on the dance floor, he would have to continue to dance.

The first drops of rain fell. Stephenson heard a voice, as yet unintelligible, amplified many times over in the damp air. It was urging the students to vote against the proposed Federation of the islands in the coming referendum. A car appeared painted in the colours of the island's opposition party. Stephenson remembered Carlton's fine waving hands.

He walked in the thin rain. Somewhere in another part of the country, perhaps even on another section of the campus, the Government's representative was blaring out reasons why the people should vote in favour of the Federation. It was just another game. Some people played games, others watched them. He was of those who watched and, he reflected, he had not chosen to be.

He was a spectator, had become, been made one. He smiled grimly to himself. He merely looked on. You did not choose the circumstances of your birth, to be born, your parents or their condition. And yet nothing in your entire life could be more important. Even death you could control. There was always the possibility of suicide. And yet had he chosen, if he could, to be born under circumstances similar to Eddie's, Thea's or even Marie's, where was the logic that enabled him to die as Eddie had, snuffed out before even he could make use of powers he had not, anyhow, asked for of anyone?

Carl, for instance, had never been to school, could not spell his name, spoke no English. He, Stephenson, was at university now. And Carl had played no part in the decision. Carl had a father; Stephenson, for all practical purposes, none at all. And yet nothing was more definite than that which the phantom, old now or dead, had given him—the quality of his hair and the colour of his skin. Yet, always, it had been their fathers that he and his friends had been to see: in an office, behind the counter of a store, behind a sewing machine in a small room full of men's clothes and bits of cloth, in the police barracks, in the Royal Gaol among wardens dressed in khaki, in a barber's shop.... They had patted his head, given a sixpence now and then, made a joke.

He was a spectator, always on the fringe, from childhood, of the groups he mixed with. In the country they called him "*ti béché*" and in the town, when they had wished to hurt, "white nigger". He was, could only have been, a spectator, supported by no weight of tradition or lineage.

The voice from the van blared on in the rain. Stephenson thought of the man responsible for that voice. Perhaps, as his own father had been, begetting him, the ageing man, whose pictures he had so often seen in the papers, did not see too clearly, or even care about the possibilities in the future of what he was doing now. Stephenson's father had been pursuing his pleasure, the opposition leader, perhaps, was pursuing his dreams of power and of being the head of a future government of the island. Stephenson wondered what would become of him in twenty, ten or even two years. Perhaps neither of the two men whose followers so loudly proclaimed and even fought each other for and against the Federation, believed anything of what they said. But there was little doubt about the results of the coming referendum. Even from his uninterested spectator's position Stephenson could see that the vote would be against the Federation and that the island would become independent alone. Carlton would be pleased he had been right.

In the long run, Stephenson thought, it made almost no sense at all. After his walk in the rain and the grey light suffused with heat, he would go back to the books he had to read which did not interest him. He would forget Eddie. His sense of loss would become dull, his anger too as well as the feeling of impotence. Eddie would become a memory, an occasional evocation, unsolicited, brought back by the walk of an unknown person in a strange street, the sound of a voice, a topic Eddie and himself had discussed or a death, in similar circumstances, read in a book or a newspaper. Stephenson and Thea would become mere occasional glimpses of what might have been or, if either were lucky enough, points of comparison, sometimes. They were like billiard balls having come together then apart each spinning forever under the impact of the other. He would forget completely neither Eddie nor Thea. Yet, already, somewhere, some woman waited. And somewhere, too, for Thea, a man was waiting.

He walked on. No crisis, no disappointment, nothing that had happened to him had stopped the flow of his life. Like a river overcoming all opposition merely by its inherent fluidity, it rolled on. Always it found its own channel, its own level. It rolled on, he thought, no longer hearing the amplified voice, as history, Federation or not, would roll on.

He walked out of the campus gates and turned left along the main road. The rain fell. Under the trees whose branches almost covered the little-used road the pattern of its fall was disturbed. Drops of water, accumulated, fell from the many leaves heavily, irregularly. Only occasionally, between their fall, he heard the light, dripping rain.

He turned left again and walked now along the road between the playing fields and the river. He could hear it out of sight below the road. Away in front of him white mist hung around the hill on which, at nights, the cluster of lights showed. The rain fell here in thin lines. There were no trees to interfere with its fall. He looked at the open fields on his left, the pavilion where he had made love to Thea, then told her he was leaving her. On the grass borders of the road the sensitive plants had closed their leaves. He did not notice that he was walking more quickly. The air felt clean, washed free of dust. He looked at the fields, at the bush between him and the river, at the distant hills and the white mist around them; and he walked for long periods without any thought at all. Once he stopped, turned, and looked the way he had come. The wet road was empty. The river roared. The falling rain made slight distinguishable sounds on his raincoat, on a leaf he went past, on a puddle in the road. Then he heard only the river and the sound of his steps. The rain had stopped. Very tiny insects hovered in the damp air in groups of thousands flitting continuously against one another. He avoided them. The damp air was suffused with heat. He walked more slowly now, his raincoat over his arm. He was perspiring.

Suddenly a shout split the air. It came from the lunatic asylum out of sight.